He had no right to question her!

Jana was trembling and her cheeks were flushed as she tried to look directly at Marco.

"Stefano kissed me," she said huskily. "Several times, and I suppose that was partly why I forgot your promise to show me the jeweled Eagle."

She almost fell into his arms when Marco reached out and pulled her against him with bruising force, smothering her small cry of surprise with the fierce hardness of his mouth....

It was only then she realized that Stefano had made her forget about the fabulous family heirloom, the Eagle, but Marco's kiss could make her forget everything and everybody, even Stefano. Uncertainly Jana wondered where she could possibly go from there.

OTHER
Harlequin Romances
by REBECCA STRATTON

Many of these titles are available at your local bookseller
or through the Harlequin Reader Service.

For a free catalogue listing all available Harlequin Romances,
send your name and address to:

HARLEQUIN READER SERVICE,
M.P.O. Box 707, Niagara Falls, N.Y. 14302
Canadian address: Stratford, Ontario, Canada N5A 6W2

or use coupon at back of book.

The Eagle of the Vincella

by

REBECCA STRATTON

Harlequin Books

TORONTO • LONDON • NEW YORK • AMSTERDAM
SYDNEY • HAMBURG • PARIS

Original hardcover edition published in 1979
by Mills & Boon Limited

ISBN 0-373-02268-9

Harlequin edition published June 1979

PRINTED IN U.S.A.

CHAPTER ONE

THE Palazzo Vincella, seen from the stern of a motor-boat making its way along a quiet backwater to the landing stage, was more than impressive, it was overwhelming and, as usual, Jana barely supressed the shiver that momentarily trickled down her back. She could not explain her reaction, nor had she attempted to so far, it was simply an automatic response to the huge and rather gloomy grandeur of the place.

In contrast to the interior, the outside of the *palazzo* had an undeniable air of neglect. The gilding on the façade had long since worn away with the passing years and had never been replaced, and the columned arcade, elegant in its day, now had a frankly run-down appearance even in the shimmering flattery of light reflected off water.

The portico had once carried a coat of arms blazoned across the front of it, but this too had become eroded with the passage of years until only the eagle, huge and threatening, still appeared as it had always done. A great creature with wings spread, looming from its stone eyrie with its curved talons grasping the pitted stone figure of a man with a sword in his hand, and its cruel beak poised to tear him to pieces. The eagle too, never failed to make Jana shudder each time she passed beneath it.

The man beside her in the stern of the boat was not likely to be so affected, for Giles Dennis was an historian and his whole outlook was centred on the past rather than the present; on the violence of history rather than the comforts of the present day. Such heraldic savagery did not disturb him because he dealt with facts that could be quite as lurid as anything Jana's imagination could conjure up.

To Jana the massive building looming about its walled courtyard had a curious air of menace. The worn stone-paved yard that echoed to their footsteps was treacherous with moss-grown crevices, and unexpectedly rough surfaces threatened to twist her ankles from under her as she stepped from the motor-boat and made her way up the ancient steps and through a low archway that gave access from the landing-stage, while her uncle paid the driver of their *motoscafo*. When he caught up with her he took her arm and smiled a little vaguely, as if he appreciated that the old place had some kind of effect on her, even though he could not understand why.

It was three days since Jana and her uncle had arrived in Venice, and their stay was to be an indefinite one, so the sooner she accustomed herself to the idea of living in a place like the Palazzo Vincella the better. That was the commonsense thought that she comforted herself with as she walked with Giles across the echoing yard.

Her first moment of discomfiture had been when she met her host for the first time. He had been a friend of her uncle's for some years, and Jana had visualised him as someone of the same calibre as Giles Dennis, and the truth had taken her rather by surprise. For one thing Count Vincella was not the greybeard she had expected, but a much younger man, and as unlike her uncle as it was possible to imagine.

Her uncle was in his early fifties but already an elderly man both in appearance and habit; completely wrapped up in his work and interested in very little beyond his own subject. He was at the moment planning a book on the art treasures of the Renaissance, and it was for this purpose that he and Jana were in Venice, for Venice was a veritable treasure-house of the Renaissance, a staggering amount of it housed under the roof of their present temporary home.

Count Vincella as well as being a qualified architect was also a keen amateur historian, and it was in the latter capacity that he had become friendly with her uncle. They had been invited to stay at the *palazzo* for as long as they wished, and their host would gladly give any help he could. More correctly the invitation had been extended to Giles Dennis, but when her uncle had mentioned that Jana was to take notes for the work she had been immediately included, although she had since suspected that her inclusion had been more polite than welcoming.

Meeting the Count had been a discomfiting experience for Jana, for not only was he not the man she had visualised him, but he was a man who made her feel quite incredibly uneasy whenever she was in his company. He was cool and formal towards her, and yet there were occasions when she felt that his tastes went beyond the merely academic, unlike her uncle, and tended towards more basic pleasures.

She could still recall her initial contact with him, and doing so brought a swift flutter of reaction from her pulse. She felt it as she crossed the tiled hall with her uncle, their footsteps tap-tapping in unison and very faintly echoed among shallow marble niches that housed alabaster and marble statues, and walls that seemed to soar upwards forever to a railed gallery from which various rooms opened off.

Portraits in massive gilt frames looked down at them and suggested haughty resignation at the intrusion of strange faces, the strong dark and autocratic features reflecting those of the present holder of the Vincella name and title. It was beautiful in an awesome and rather chilling way, and it struck Jana as ice-cold after the sunshine outside, so that she actually did shiver this time.

Her uncle seldom had much to say unless it concerned his

current interest, but Jana did not take his silence amiss, for she was used to it. They had a rapport that was perhaps not immediately obvious to anyone else, but which meant a lot to Jana. She had been close to her uncle ever since she had become part of his bachelor household after her parents died, and she knew that he was not completely unaware of some slight discomfiture on her part, although he was probably puzzled by it. He was not a demonstrative man, but he was a warmly affectionate one in his way, and Jana loved him.

'You have our notes safely, my dear?'

He asked the question as they climbed the wide marble staircase to the gallery on the first floor, and Jana smiled. 'Yes, I have them right here, Giles.' She tapped the satchel-handbag she carried slung from her shoulder. 'Quite safe.'

It was flattering of him to refer to them as 'our notes', for in fact she did no more than take down what her uncle told her, and then later transcribe them into typed notes, but it was nice to feel part of the project, and she enjoyed working with him. Even the Count, she thought, recognised her as an essential part of the project, and as such, less of a distraction that she would otherwise have been.

At the top of the staircase an archway led through to a door, panelled and gilded as so much of the interior of the *palazzo* was, and even after three days Jana experienced a curious flutter of apprehension when they walked through into the main *sala* and the presence of their host. It was automatic to busy her hands with taking out the bulky note-book full of her uncle's instructions, while Count Vincella got up out of his chair, rather than look directly at him.

Even in a room as big as this one, filled with Baroque extravagance, he seemed to dominate, and once more her pulse fluttered uneasily. 'Ah, my friend, some wine, eh?' Jana could forgive him almost anything for his obvious affection for her uncle, even though her own reception was noticably less fulsome. '*Signorina?*'

'Yes, thank you.'

She subsided into an armchair while the Count went to pour them drinks, and grew annoyed with her own clumsiness when she almost spilled the wine trying to change her notebook to the other hand before she took it. Her uncle apparently noticed nothing, but she could hardly miss the swift elevation of one black brow in comment on her clumsiness as their host waited for her to dispose of the book and take her drink from him.

'Please take your time, *signorina*.'

He was politeness itself, but still Jana flushed with embarrassment because she felt he found her fumblingly inadequate. Her uncle was sipping the rather fine red wine with an absent air and interested in nothing, as always, but the progress he had made during the morning. He picked up the notebook from where she had put it on a stool between their two chairs, and handed it to his friend, anxious to have his opinion on their quite gruelling morning's walking.

'You will see we've made quite good progress, Marco. I've almost walked poor Jana off her feet, haven't I, my dear?'

'Not at all, I loved it!'

The Count did not sit down again himself, but balanced easily on the edge of a table while he flicked through the pages of her notebook, taking note of the various small sketches she had made to augment her uncle's remarks. Thus seated, at an angle to her, Jana was able to study him without herself being observed.

Marco Gaspare Fabriano was the fourteenth Conte di Vincella, but preferred to be called simply *signore* rather than by his title, a modest affectation that did not fit in at all with Jana's reading of his character. He was, she had soon decided, every bit as proud of his ancient line as any of his forebears must have been.

He was a man difficult to date, but she guessed he was somewhere between thirty and forty; tall and black-haired and with deep brown eyes between thick short lashes. His features were handsome in a strong and very masculine way and there was, she always felt, a suggestion of cruelty in the wide firm mouth, although she could not have said why she was so convinced of that.

He wore a white silk shirt, open at the neck to reveal a strong brown throat, and a firm jaw gave a hint of ruthlessness. A light jacket had been discarded in favour of shirt-sleeves, and brown well-cut slacks showed long muscular legs. He was lean-hipped and broad-shouldered and shatteringly masculine as he sat with one foot swinging casually while he attempted to interpret Jana's shorthand.

Turning to face her suddenly, he caught her off guard, and for a moment she caught a glimpse of amusement in the glittering darkness of his eyes. Holding out the notebook to her, he smiled, taking drink from his wine glass before he spoke. 'You are a very passable artist, *signorina*, but I cannot make anything of your notes. Perhaps when you have them typed I shall find them more easily understandable.'

'Oh, but of course you will!' She took back the proffered book and gave her uncle a swift look of reproach from the corner of her eye. 'No one else is expected to be able to read them in this form; Giles must have known that!'

His comment on her artistic ability was unexpected and flattering, for as an architect himself he was well qualified to judge. It was sincere too, she was sure of it, for he was not the kind of man to pass judgment lightly. Taking her book from him, she once more met his eyes for a moment and was appalled to realise how much such a brief contact could affect her confidence. It was something she was not accustomed to experiencing with the men she normally met, but it was yet another reason for her wariness of Count Vincella.

'You find the typewriter you have suitable for your purpose?'

There was something almost beautiful about the perfectly modulated voice speaking its pedantic English. It was a quality that she always admired in a man, and in some perverse way it made her wish that Count Vincella did not possess it. The typewriter had appeared on her borrowed desk the morning after her arrival and appeared to be brand new, so that she wondered if it had been purchased especially for the convenience of his old friend. Such extravagant gestures were well within his means, she knew, and not out of character for the man as she saw him. But however she felt about his extravagance, it was a good machine.

'It's perfect, thank you, *signore*, and it was very good of you to provide it.'

'Not at all, *signorina*. I have promised all possible help to my old friend, Giles, and the clear transcription of his notes is of importance to his work, is it not, my friend?'

'Oh, most important!' Giles smiled at him a little vaguely, his mind busy with some aspect of his project no doubt.

The Count left his seat on the table edge and took the armchair immediately opposite Jana's, crossing one long leg over the other and reaching for a cigarette from the box beside him. He knew her uncle did not smoke, but he had never bothered to ask whether Jana did or not, although possibly her uncle had told him she didn't. He lit the cigarette and sent a spiral of smoke curling towards the high vaulted ceiling before he spoke again, cigarette and wine glass both held in one hand while the other smoothed over the knee of his immaculate slacks.

'I hope it will not prove too distracting for you to have some members of my family here for a few days,' he said, and Giles looked at him with a vague frown.

'If we're in the way, my dear chap——'

'Not at all,' the Count denied smoothly and hastily, 'I think only of your comfort, my friend.'

'But of course you must have your family here, Marco. Jana and I don't expect to be treated like honoured guests all the time, you know. This is your home and you mustn't let us disturb your way of life—no, indeed you mustn't!'

'I shall not be in the least disturbed however long you stay.' That smooth and incredibly soothing voice reassured her uncle as it was meant to, and a half-smile recognised his willingness to be reassured. A swift glance at Jana from the concealment of those short, thick lashes drew her back into the conversation. 'My cousin and her son are coming here for a short time while they are in Venice and I cannot but anticipate some—disturbance for Signorina Dennis when Stefano arrives. However, I am sure the *signorina* is accustomed to dealing with the advances of amorous young men, is that not so, *signorina*?'

Blandly unconcerned and confident that he knew what he was talking about, Giles Dennis laughed and waved a careless hand. 'Oh, don't worry about that, Marco. Jana isn't that easily distracted from something she's really interested in, are you, my dear?'

His attitude and his assurances were naïve and the Count knew it, his eyes said as much when he looked across at Jana through a pall of smoke from his cigarette, so that when she answered it was with a lot less confidence than her uncle did.

'I'm not very easily distracted as a rule, Giles, so I doubt if I will be in this instance.'

A soft deep sound of laughter greeted her reply, and it startled her for a moment because it was unexpected. 'You have yet to meet my young cousin, *signorina*—we shall see how difficult you are to distract after Stefano arrives!'

Jana had not expected the visitors to arrive quite so soon, and as she changed for dinner that evening she wondered if the Count himself had been unaware of their coming until that morning. It seemed odd in the circumstances that he had not said at least a word or two to her uncle, if he had known, for they were very good friends.

Stefano, whoever he might prove to be, sounded as if he had a reputation as far as women were concerned, but that was something that Jana could quite easily accept in the circumstances, knowing his relationship to their host. Unless she had been doing Marco Vincella an injustice these past three days, he was no mean exponent in that direction himself.

It was impossible to remain unaware of his frequent studies of her whenever she was in his company, and there was no mistaking the meaning in those dark and very expressive eyes no matter how cool and formal his manner might be. She was not unaccustomed to the admiration of the opposite sex, and only someone as unworldly and single-minded as her uncle could fail to be aware of the meaning behind those long and speculative studies.

Her reflection was encouraging, as always, and the deep blue dress she wore did wonders for her eyes as well as showing off the golden overtones in her hair. Just another shade or two and it could have been called sandy, but as it was it had a golden sheen that was stunning when combined with a creamy complexion and thick brown lashes. Jana sometimes wished she was a little taller, but mostly her diminutive stature was an advantage, and she was subject to all kinds of old-fashioned courtesies from the opposite sex, so that for the most part she was content to have things as they were.

She took a moment to take in the view from her bedroom window, as she most often did whenever she had the opportunity. The view was of rooftops and water, merged and misted by the softening light of late evening; of exquisite cupolas and spires, turrets and campaniles clustered in breathtaking confusion among the snaking scribble of canals that ducked under bridges and curled out of sight, weaving around the architecture of mingled centuries. Jana already felt something of the magic of Venice, and when she stopped to think about it, she should be grateful to Count Vincella for giving her the privilege of this view each morning and evening.

Thinking she caught the sound of voices, she turned from the window and listened for a moment. She had thought she heard someone arrive earlier, when she was typing out Giles' notes, and the strange voices suggested she had been right—the expected visitors had evidently arrived in time to join them for dinner.

She recognised her uncle's voice among the unmistakably Italian ones that reached her from the echoing gallery outside her door. His atrocious Italian was easily identifiable and, while she took a last glimpse in the mirror, the conversation changed into English. Evidently his attempts were unintelligible to the newcomers too.

When she opened her bedroom door she found herself almost in the centre of the group; her uncle and a man and woman she did not know. Giles took her arm, nervously, he was always a little anxious with strangers. 'Jana, my dear, I'm so glad you're here! Let me introduce you.'

They stood grouped on the wide carpeted gallery under the bright yellow light of a crystal chandelier and Jana took a swift, surreptitious survey while her uncle performed introductions in his quick, anxious fashion. 'May I introduce my niece, Jana Dennis: Jana, this is Signora Abrizzi and her son, Signor Stefano Abrizzi—Marco's family.'

'Marco's cousins, *signorina*; *felice di conoscerla*!'

In fact Signora Abrizzi was so much like their host that it was not difficult to believe their relationship, even without the Signora's emphasis. She was tall for a woman, but perhaps not quite so dark as he was, and elegantly beautiful, with an excellent figure and glossy black hair that she wore short and straight in a swinging bob that framed her face. Looking at her Jana would have guessed she was no more than thirty-four or five, but Stefano Abrizzi looked to be about Jana's own age, and a woman of that age was unlikely to be mother to a young man of twenty-two.

Stefano, her son, was dark, good-looking and well aware of the fact that he was a very attractive young man. He had huge dark eyes that immediately settled on Jana and did not leave her face all the time her uncle was introducing her to his mother and himself. Seizing her hand in both his, he conveyed it to his lips while he murmured in Italian.

'*Sono molto lieto di fare la sua conoscenza, signorina!* I am very pleased to meet with you. My cousin has not prepared me for such a delightful surprise!' He retained his hold on her hand, and Jana felt no compulsion at the moment to do anything about it. 'He tells us only that there is an English friend and his niece staying here who are to write a book on the Renaissance history, so—what can I imagine from this, *signorina*, eh?'

He shrugged expressive shoulders, and it was so obvious what he had imagined that Jana could do nothing about the smile that made her eyes sparkle with mischief. 'An elderly lady in twin-set and pearls?' she suggested, and he pulled a wry face.

'Something of this sort, *signorina*. The history writing and the interest in ancient things—it is natural, eh?'

'Oh, but surely, Signor Abrizzi, that image of the English woman disappeared with the onset of cheap travel, didn't it?'

Signora Abrizzi obviously appreciated the teasing her son was receiving, and she was smiling, but her son looked a little taken aback and as if he was not used to being laughed at, however goodnaturedly. He took Jana's arm as they started once more towards the stairs, and he obviously meant to make a good impression, though perhaps he was doing himself an injustice by not realising how much he had already impressed her.

'You are staying here for a long time, *signorina*?'

Somehow he had contrived to keep them some distance behind his mother and Giles, and he was tall enough so that when he bent his head to speak to her it gave the impression of intimacy. His hand held her arm only lightly, but it was a lingering touch that conveyed as much as the dark warmth of his eyes did when she looked up at him as they started downstairs. It was becoming more apparent every second just how right the Count had been to anticipate her being distracted, and she wondered if he had anticipated finding the situation amusing.

'Count Vincella has very kindly told my uncle that we can stay for as long as we need to to complete Giles' notes, so we may be here a month or so. Unless,' she added hastily, 'the Count gets tired of having us here or finds it inconvenient.'

'Ah no, he will most assuredly not do that, Signorina Dennis!' For a second the dark eyes surveyed her curiously. 'You surely do not think that he would, eh?'

Aware that there was some significant implication in the question, Jana hastily gave her attention to watching the wide marble steps they were descending, one hand holding on to the balustrade, the other lifting the hem of her long skirt to avoid treading on it. 'We've only been here three days, *signore*, I can't really claim to know the Count all that well.'

'Ah, but you know him for the man he is, eh?'

It was a situation that Jana would have given much to avoid. A discussion of her host's character was the last thing she desired, especially with a man she had met only a matter of minutes ago and who was related to him. She looked down anxiously at the heads of her uncle and Signora Abrizza and wished there was some polite way of changing places with the Signora—her uncle did not have the same dismaying ability to suspect what was going on in her mind as Stefano Abrizzi seemed to.

'I really can't pass an opinion on anyone on such short acquaintance, *signore*, and I don't think I should be discussing Count Vincella with you.'

She thought she had offended him for a moment, for he was quiet, but men like Stefano Abrizzi are not easily subdued, she should have known that, and a moment later he was once more speaking close to her ear, though the subject was completely changed. Dropped as if it had never been mentioned.

'Mamma and I will be staying here for several weeks I hope,' he informed her. 'I hope that you and I may become good friends in that time, Signorina Dennis, eh?'

As far as Jana could remember the count had mentioned a stay of only a few days, and she wondered if he knew of his cousin's plans yet, or if Stefano had only just decided that it would suit him better to stay longer, without consulting anybody else.

'I hope so, Signor Abrizzi,' she said, and the hand on her arm gave just the slightest squeeze.

'I will make your stay very enjoyable, I promise, *signorina*. We shall visit the *romantico* places, eh? Together, just you and I!'

It all sounded very inviting, Jana allowed, but she reminded herself that she was in no position to agree to sightseeing tours with Stefano Abrizzi when she was there to assist her uncle with his project. She shook her head and smiled, even though she was being quite blatantly coaxed by a finger-tip tracing around the inner softness of her wrist.

'I'm going to be very busy while I'm here, Signor Abrizzi.' She saw his frown from the corner of her eye, and guessed he was not used to being refused. 'My reason for coming was to help my uncle gather material for his book, and I go with him most days—there isn't very much free time, I'm afraid.'

'Then I will speak to your uncle and ask that he release you to my care for a few hours each day, *mia cara signorina*.' He raised the hand nearest to him and kissed the finger-tips lightly, a mere brush with his lips but enough to arouse all kinds of alarming responses in Jana's susceptible emotions. 'You will like that!'

He had no doubt that she would like it, and Jana could hardly admit he was wrong, but she did not see her uncle taking quite the same view of it. Not that he would begrudge her the pleasure of going around with Stefano Abrizzi, but he would simply not understand how she could wish to, when there were so many more exciting hours to be had exploring the historic beauties of Venice with him.

And Count Vincella's view might not be favourable either. She had been invited to the *palazzo* to stay because she was essential to her uncle's work, but he might not be as welcoming if she should suddenly abandon her work for the company of his cousin, and make her stay more a holiday.

'It sounds very tempting,' she told Stefano as they walked down into the chillingly massive hall and crossed towards a room she had not yet seen into. 'But I'm here to help my uncle, Signor Abrizzi, and I'm afraid he couldn't spare me. I take notes as he studies the places he wishes to mention and make small sketches, then I type out the notes and Giles and the Count go through them together. He'd find it very difficult to manage without me and I can't hinder him by taking any amount of time off.'

Stefano Abrizzi murmured something in Italian, and when Jana looked at him from the corner of her eye, there was a definitely sulky look on his good-looking face, though she guessed it would not stay there for long. For one thing he would realise how much it marred his good looks, and for another she guessed he was not the kind of man to give up anything he wanted, any more than his autocratic cousin was. He would find some way of having his way, she would have sworn to it.

He escorted her into the *grande sala de pranzo* in the wake of her uncle and Signora Abrizzi, and the room itself took Jana's breath away. During the three days that she and her uncle had been there it had not been used, but apparently with the advent of two more guests, the Count had decided to open up the grand dining-room, and their meal was set in an atmosphere of baroque splendour.

It was so huge that five people scarcely disturbed its pall of stillness, although Jana could imagine it filled with people in the old days of the Vincellas. Venetian mirrors lined its walls between gilded panels and scrolled candle-holders, and the furniture was in period; elegant and heavily gilded and upholstered in deep red velvet. Huge crystal chandeliers hung overhead, glittering like diamonds in their own light, and scattering sparkles of movement over everything on the long table.

The Count was already waiting for them when they went in, and he provided pre-dinner drinks with a smile that suggested he was well pleased with himself about the impression the room made. He looked darker than ever in a white dinner jacket, and the brilliance of the chandeliers gave a depth and glitter to his dark eyes that made them look like polished jet.

One long brown hand held a wine glass and he smiled over its rim at the small company of guests. 'Forgive my ostentation, my friends, but I wished to amuse my good friend Giles with this show of baroque magnificence. Giles, you are writing about the Renaissance, but this is to show you what followed that exquisite period; how taste ran wild after so much beauty!'

Giles, as it happened, was interested and he peered about him with his slightly short-sighted eyes, as he might have done in a museum or a gallery. 'My dear Marco, I am familiar with the period, though I must say that to actually *live* among such surroundings is a trifle—er—breathtaking.'

The Count was obviously enjoying himself, and laughter brought a softer more youthful look to his strong face, so that Jana found herself fascinated anew by yet another aspect of the man. While he sipped his aperitif he pointed out various features of the huge room, showing delight in the sheer extravagance of the place.

It abounded with gilding and scrollwork. A frescoed ceiling showing the pleasures of country life in explicit detail but with exquisite workmanship was framed in curlicues, heavily gilded, and the walls were hung with paintings by masters of the period; Canaletto and Guardi appearing between the gilded panels and the huge mirrors. It was dazzling and overpowering, and yet it had a grandeur that was impressive for all its extravagance, and it was staggering in its richness.

Jana gazed upwards at the frescoes for several minutes, dazed by the skilful execution rather than the frankness of the subjects, and she brought her gaze back to earth once more only to find herself looking directly at Count Vincella. The dark eyes held hers for a long moment before she managed to look away, and her pulse rate increased rapidly in those few moments, so that she held her wine glass tightly between both hands.

'You do not like the frescoes, Signorina Dennis?'

His question was bound to bring all eyes in her direction,

and Jana wished she was able to put on a bolder face. Whether or not he had meant to embarrass her, he had succeeded in doing so, and she was appalled to realise how much her hands were trembling as they clasped the stem of her glass.

'They're wonderful work,' she said in her coolest voice. 'They're very similar to those at the Villa Valmarana, near Vincenza, aren't they? Although I would say that these are a slightly later date.'

A glittering gleam in the dark eyes congratulated her on both her knowledge and her panache, and he inclined his head slightly. 'Not so much later that it is easy for a layman to recognise, *signorina*—I must compliment you on your knowledge.'

Smiling across at her uncle, Jana gave credit where it was due. 'I had a good instructor,' she said. 'But thank you anyway, *signore*.'

Heaven knew why he had the effect he did, especially when she had someone like Stefano standing beside her; young and good-looking and prepared to pay her all the compliments she could want. The Count's eyes watched her still, dark and speculative and disturbingly bright in that strongly handsome face.

'You delight in such surroundings as these?'

It took her a moment or two to realise that he had some-how gravitated towards her and Stefano, and he barely raised his voice when he asked the question, so that Jana did no more than nod her head to agree. Taking another drink from his glass, he savoured the wine on his lips while he studied her from beneath the cover of his short thick lashes, smudged like shadows on high smooth cheekbones.

'You would fit well into such a scene, *signorina*.' His gaze flicked swiftly over her golden hair and the soft warmth of her mouth, tremulous and uncertain. 'Hmm?'

Her fingers tightened just that fraction too much and the

stem of her glass snapped between them, making her cry out when the sharp fragments cut into her flesh. She heard Stefano Abrizzi murmur something anxiously in Italian and she herself stared at the blood that came running from her fingers as if she did not believe it was happening, then suddenly there was a strong hand around her wrist, holding out the hand that had been cut while a spotless white handkerchief was wrapped carefully about her fingers.

She made a small murmur of protest more by instinct than for any other reason, but the hand remained, and the handkerchief bound her fingers together tightly. Then she felt her knees shaking as if they would not go on supporting her and there was a hand in the small of her back, then an arm around her waist as she made her way towards one of the gilded chairs against the wall.

'Jana? You must sit for a moment until the fainting has passed! Come!' She was seated firmly on the chair and her head bowed towards her knees, held there by that firm hand which was now on the back of her neck.

It occurred to her suddenly what a fool she was, behaving as if she had been badly hurt, when all she had done was to cut herself on a broken glass. The slight dizziness was passing now and she raised her head in opposition to the hand on her neck. Lifting her face, she looked straight into Count Vincella's dark eyes once more, and for the first time realised that he was capable of compassion.

'You are feeling better?' He let her lift her head, but the hand remained on the nape of her neck and she was staggeringly conscious of his nearness. He looked at his cousin and held out an imperious hand. 'Some wine for the *signorina*, Stefano, *per piacere*!'

'I'm all right, *signore*, really I'm quite all right now.'

'Nevertheless,' the Count decreed, 'you will drink a little wine, and then we shall see what is to be done about your hand.'

'It's stopped bleeding and it's much better!'

The firm mouth smiled and he bent close to press the glass of wine into her good hand when Stefano brought it, the gleaming dark eyes holding hers for long enough to bring colour to her cheeks. 'You will not go without your dinner, *piccina*, do not worry!'

Wishing that Giles was not always so much at a loss when things went slightly wrong, Jana obediently sipped some of the wine he insisted she have, while the Count stood over her as if he meant to see that she drank it all. No one seemed to even think of opposing him, and in the circumstances she supposed it was understandable, but she was not badly hurt and she hated to make a fuss.

'I'm not worrying about my dinner, *signore*, but about *yours*. If I can keep this handkerchief on my hand, you needn't bother about it any more for the moment.'

For a moment he said nothing, but there was a slight narrowing of those expressive eyes for a moment before he smiled; a small and rather tight smile. '*Benissimo!*' He yielded at last, and stood up straight looking down at her for a moment, catching her eye when Jana would have avoided the contact. 'You are stubborn, *piccina*, I think, eh?' He reached down and took the wine glass from her and in doing so his long hard fingers brushed hers for a second while he watched her face flush with colour once more. 'You will be unable to work for several days until your hand heals, so it is as well that Stefano is here, eh?'

For some reason she could not fathom, Jana did not like his casual assignment of her to his young cousin, and she looked down again hastily, seeking to still the inexplicable resentment she felt. 'Just as well,' she agreed.

CHAPTER TWO

JANA considered it quite unnecessary for her to take time off from her duties because of the cuts on her hand, and she said so at breakfast the following morning. Stefano Abrizzi had suggested that as she was incapacitated they might take his cousin's motorlaunch as far as St Mark's Square and then walk from there; her refusal on the grounds that she was quite able to work not only surprised him but displeased him too, judging by his frown.

'But last night you injured your hand on broken glass, *signorina*,' he insisted. 'It is not good that you do not rest it for a few days, eh?'

'It really isn't necessary, *signore*.' Jana extended her hand for him to see the small adhesive plasters that were all she had found necessary this morning, on two of her fingers. 'You see,' she told him with a smile, 'I have only two very minor cuts; the rest weren't even serious enough to cover with plaster this morning.'

'But last night,' Stefano insisted with a frown. 'So much blood, *signorina*, and you almost fainted.'

It was embarrassing being reminded of that incident, and Jana wished she could have carried it off with the panache she wanted to. If she had not responded so irrationally to that half-mocking manner of the Count's it would not have happened, but it had, and both Stefano and his mother had been there to see how silly she had been. Instead of looking at him, she resumed her breakfast of hot rolls, butter and honey, and ignored his look of injured reproach.

'I'm a coward where blood is concerned, *signore*, and I made a complete idiot of myself last night.' She included

24

Signora Abrizzi in her smile. 'I'm sorry I made such a scene, you must think me very silly.'

'Nothing of the kind, *signorina*,' Signora Abrazzi assured her with a hint of a smile that suggested she had at least an inkling of what had brought on that sudden nervousness and tightened her grip on the stem of her glass until it snapped. 'It is fortunate that no worse damage was done to your hand.'

Aware that the Count was watching but not at the moment taking part in the conversation, Jana once more flicked her plastered fingers and smiled ruefully. 'As you see, nothing more than two small plasters; I can go out with Giles as usual this morning.'

From the other end of the table Count Vincella's dark eyes sought and held Jana's until she could sustain the contact no longer, then he half-smiled before making his own opinion known in that stunningly affecting voice. 'You have recovered remarkably quickly, Signorina Dennis, but I cannot imagine that Giles would object to your taking a few hours from your secretarial duties to see a little of Venice in the company of my cousin. If he was here I am sure he would endorse what I say unhesitatingly.'

It only now occurred to Jana to wonder why in fact her uncle had not yet put in an appearance when he was usually so early getting up. She glanced over her shoulder and frowned, a curious sense of uneasiness stirring in her when she saw no sign of him. 'I can't think why Giles *isn't* here,' she said thoughtfully. 'It's not like him to be so late getting up, he's usually such an early riser.'

Neither Stefano nor Signora Abrizzi seemed to sense anything amiss, but Jana sensed that the Count was watching her as he leaned with one elbow resting on the table while he sipped his coffee. After a moment or two his gaze too followed the direction of Jana's and he narrowed his eyes slightly.

'I have observed in the past three days that Giles is usually around in the morning before anyone else,' he remarked, obviously musing on the fact. 'Is it his habit to rise early every morning, *signorina*?'

'Always.' The niggle of uneasiness persisted, and yet she could think of no real reason for it.

'And you are troubled by his not doing so this morning, eh?'

She hated to confess as much, and hesitated. If Giles was simply oversleeping she would feel very foolish if she made a fuss about it, and for that reason she did not immediately reply. 'I'm not exactly troubled by it, *signore*,' she allowed after a moment or two, 'but it isn't like Giles to oversleep.'

'He was quite well when you saw him last night?'

Jana nodded, then remembered that when she went to bed last night she had left her uncle in the Count's company; discussing some aspect of architecture that she knew nothing about, although both men were apparently completely involved in it. 'I left him in the library with you last night, *signore*, if you remember. I didn't notice anything wrong then.'

'Ah, *sì, sì*, so you did!' The Count's frown deepened for a moment, then he shook his head. 'But no, he seemed tired, and he complained of being so, but he said nothing of being unwell.' Putting down his coffee cup, he looked at Jana questioningly for a moment, then laughed and shook his head once more. 'Ah, but we make much of nothing, eh? A man sleeps late—why should he be ill? A different climate, too much wine, almost anything could account for this, hah?'

'Yes, of course! He's probably just sleeping late, as you say.'

She got on with her breakfast again, and was conscious of Stefano Abrizzi casting her curious and reproachful looks every so often, although he said nothing more about her taking time off. But that small niggle of doubt would not be completely subdued, she discovered, and after a while Giles' continued absence began to make her uneasy once more. Glancing along to the end of the table, she looked at the Count apologetically as she started to get to her feet.

'If you'll excuse me, *signore*, I'll go and see where Giles has got to.' She placed a hand on her stomach where the niggling sensation seemed to originate, and laughed a little sheepishly. 'I expect I'm being a complete idiot, but I have a—a funny kind of feeling and I'd like to put my mind at rest, if you'll please excuse me.'

'*Naturalmente, signorina.*' The Count had half risen from his chair and for a moment Jana caught a glimpse of the compassion she had seen in his eyes last night, when she had hurt her hand. It was as unexpected now as it had been then, and it gave her a curiously comfortable feeling that she would never have attributed to anything that Count Vincella did. 'I hope that we are wrong, eh?'

That intimate 'we' too seemed to suggest that he shared her slight apprehension, and Jana puzzled yet again over the complex character of the man. 'I hope so,' she agreed a little breathlessly.

She crossed the hall and started up the carpeted marble staircase, the treads muffling her footsteps so that it seemed oddly silent after hearing them tap-tapping across the tiled floor. And it enabled her to catch the sound of voices before she reached her uncle's room, making her hurry without quite understanding her own sudden sense of urgency. She was almost there when one of the maids came scurrying from the room, and Jana needed only a glance at the girl's face to know that something was wrong.

'What is it?' She grasped the girl's arm, looking past her through the partly open door and half afraid of what she might see, praying that this was one of the servants who spoke English. '*Cosa c'è?*'

'*Il signore,*' the girl told her, struggling to make herself understood. 'Giacomo say for me to bring *caffè* because *il signore* does not appear like always, and when I get here——'

'Giles!' She thrust the girl to one side and pushed open Giles' door. 'Giles, what's wrong, are you——' She stopped short when she recognised one of the other servants standing beside the bed, his brown face showing a hint of sheepishness as well as anxiety when he saw her.

'*Buon giorno, signorina.*'

'Giacomo, what is it? What's wrong with my uncle?'

The man shrugged, spreading his hands helplessly, but standing back so that Jana could come past him and see for herself, and she caught her breath when she looked down into Giles' face. He was pale, almost grey in his pallor, and perspiration stood out on his forehead and his upper lip; his eyes were barely more than slits so that he took a moment or two before he recognised her. She needed no expert advice to tell her that her uncle was a very sick man indeed, and she turned to Giacomo again, placing a hand on her uncle's forehead as she did so.

'He needs a doctor quickly, Giacomo, will you please send for one? My Italian isn't very good, and——'

'*Sì, signorina,* I have already sent Sophia to tell *il Conte* that a *dottore* is needed.'

'But we need a doctor *at once,* not when the Count gets here! Please get on the telephone and get one here as quickly as possible!'

'*Sì, sì, signorina!*'

The man made no more ado, but hurried off, and Jana hoped he would do as she said and not wait for permission from his employer. Her mind was put at rest when she heard the faint ping of a telephone only a moment or so later, and she allowed herself a brief sigh of relief. Using a clean handkerchief, she wet it under the cold water tap in

the adjoining bathroom, then pressed it gently over Giles'
brow. But he moaned faintly when she bent over him and
her eyes were darkly anxious as she waited for someone else
to come. She felt so horribly helpless, and she hated it.

'Giles. Giles, are you in bad pain?'

He opened his eyes a little, but they were mere slits in
the grey-tinged face, and she was appalled at the change in
him since last night when she had left him with the Count
in the library. She remembered that he had looked rather
tired, as Count Vincella had said, but he had not complained of pain, and he never had a very high colour.

It was strange that neither she nor the Count had noticed
anything amiss apart from the tiredness, and she wondered
if they had both overlooked signs that should have given
them a clue, but could think of none. He had one hand
restlessly rubbing over the lower right-hand side of his
stomach, she noticed, and Jana licked her lips anxiously
when a new and more worrying possibility occurred to her.

She had immediately thought of possible food-poisoning,
for she could have understood that to some extent. Her
uncle was normally rather a meagre eater and their meal
last night had been as sumptuous as their surroundings; so
much rich food could have upset him more readily than it
had her, but that stroking hand seemed to suggest a possible
appendicitis, and that was much more serious. His voice too
was small and incredibly weak, barely more than a whisper,
so that she tried to shush him to silence before he said too
much and overtaxed his strength.

'I'm—I'm afraid I have appendicitis, my dear—I'm so
sorry.'

'Oh, Giles!' She held on to his hand tightly, and bent to
kiss his cheek, feeling a sudden urgent need to cry choking
in her throat as she fought against yielding to it. 'You don't
have anything to apologise for, especially to me—you can't
help being ill. I've asked Giacomo to ring for a doctor; he'll

soon have you feeling better. Now please don't worry, and don't talk.'

There was a dull sheen on his eyes that she did not like at all but apparently he felt he must try and say something else, for all it cost him in effort. 'Marco will——' he began, and Jana pressed a gentle but firm finger over his lips to silence him.

'Marco is as concerned about you as I am—he knows you're never late coming down to breakfast, just as I do.'

'Such a nuisance,' her uncle whispered. 'In his home, I didn't——'

'Oh, but you couldn't help being taken ill in his house, Giles, Marco will understand that, he's a reasonable man. What's more,' she added with an encouraging smile, 'he's a very compassionate man, he isn't going to blame you for anything.' She bent to kiss his cheek once more and failed to realise that someone else had come into the room as she did so. 'Now keep quiet and wait for the doctor.'

'Giles?' The unmistakable voice spoke so close behind her that Jana was startled and turned swiftly, only to find her hands caught in one strong brown one that imprisoned hers for a moment against the comforting breadth of his chest, while he looked down into her face. 'What is wrong?' He put her aside gently without waiting for her reply, then pressed past her to stand beside the bed, looking down at the grey tinged features and perspiring forehead gravely. '*Dio mio*, my poor old friend! What has happened to you?'

'He—it seems as if he might have appendicitis,' Jana ventured, the words caught in her throat, and the Count turned to her again, noting the anxious darkness in her eyes and the slight tremor of her lips. 'I hope it isn't, but it looks so very much like it, I——'

She shook her head on the rest of the sentence and once more he reached out and squeezed her hand briefly. 'The *dottore* will soon tell us what is wrong, *piccina*, in the meantime do not distress yourself too much, eh? Everything will be done that will help him, you may be sure of it.'

'I asked Giacomo to ring for a doctor.' Jana was not sure just how he was going to take to the idea of her giving instructions to his servants, but in fact he merely nodded his head approvingly.

'*Sì*, I have seen Giacomo; you acted with promptitude, *signorina*. I came as soon as Sophia told me what had happened, it was a relief to know that the doctor was already on call.'

'Marco.'

A wavering hand reached up from the bed and touched his arm, and the Count immediately bent over her uncle, his expression one of gentle compassion. '*Sì*, *sì*, my old friend?'

'Marco.' The thin voice wavered as Giles struggled to say what he wanted to. 'Please—you'll see that Jana is all right, won't you? You'll see that she——'

'*Sì*, *sì*, *sì*, my friend, I will take good care of Jana for you until you are back with us again, do not concern yourself, eh?' He glanced at Jana for a second and smiled. 'She will be quite safe with me, Giles, have no fear.'

It was startling for a moment to realise that they were discussing her as if she was too young to know her own mind or to take care of herself, and just for a second or two she resented it. But then she realised that her uncle at least was genuinely concerned about her, he genuinely believed she was incapable of managing alone in a strange country, and in the circumstances she had to appreciate the Count's willingness to reassure him.

'Thank you!' Giles' relief was so obvious that Jana felt another lump in her throat as she moved nearer to him, pressing herself between the Count's tall figure and the edge of the bed to get to him. 'Jana, my dear, you'll be all

right with Marco, and please don't worry about me if I
have to go away for a while.'

'I'll be fine, Giles, honestly, don't worry about me.'

'You will remember——'

'*Il dottore!*'

The Count's murmured statement cut him short, and he
went striding out of the room in search of the doctor, while
Jana looked down at her uncle in sudden apprehension, lest
he should be even worse than she feared, her hand holding
tightly to his. Until you come back to us, the Count had
said, and Giles himself had anticipated going away but it
hadn't really come home to Jana until now that he would
almost certainly be going into hospital, and for a second she
felt completely at a loss.

She could hear voices coming along the gallery, one of
them unmistakably the Count's, the other almost certainly
the doctor's, and her fingers squeezed her uncle's tightly
while she listened. Then she turned and gave him a smile,
though it did not quite reach her eyes, which still had that
dark anxious look that had aroused Marco's sympathy.

'I think the doctor is here, Giles, we'll soon know what's
wrong now.'

Her uncle said nothing, but there was a responsive pressure from his fingers and the door opened again a moment
afterwards to admit Marco and a tall grey-haired man in
glasses. The newcomer glanced at his patient, then at Jana,
and she automatically moved away from the bed, leaving
the way clear for him. As if he knew exactly how she was
feeling, the Count opened the door for her, catching and
holding her hand for a moment as she passed him, and
pressing her fingers in his while he looked at her steadily,
showing no sign in his eyes of the smile that touched his
straight firm mouth.

'I'd better leave while the doctor examines him, hadn't
I?'

'I think that it would be better so.' He squeezed her fingers before letting them go, and again that trace of a smile hovered about his mouth to encourage her. 'And please do not worry too much, Jana, eh? Have I not promised to care for you while your uncle is ill?' A long forefinger traced a light firm line down her cheek before she was dismissed from the room. 'I will come and tell you what is to happen immediately I know myself—I promise. *D'accordo?*'

With a last glance at the doctor bending over his patient, Jana nodded. There was nothing else she could do for him, but she wished she did not feel so very dependent upon Count Vincella. 'Thank you, *signore.*'

When she made her way back to the breakfast table she found Stefano and Signora Abrizzi still sitting there looking as if nothing was any different, and it took Jana a moment to realise that they had not received the same kind of shock that she had herself, they were so far unaffected by what had happened.

Signora Abrizzi looked up as Jana came into the room, and for a moment Jana registered the same look of compassion in her eyes that she had seen in Marco's; her son, on the other hand, showed rather more curiosity than concern, which on reflection was more natural in a young man, untouched by strangers about him.

'How is your poor uncle, *signorina*?' Signora Abrizzi was pouring her coffee and passed it to her as she asked the question. 'Sophia brought the news that he was ill; is it very serious, *signorina*?'

'There's a possibility it might be appendicitis.' Jana was appalled to realise how shaky her voice was, and she took a hasty sip of her coffee before she went on, conscious of the Signora's sympathy and grateful for it. 'The doctor's with him now, and Marco. Giles is used to him and I couldn't very well stay, not——' She used her hands in a curiously helpless gesture. 'He's promised to let me know as soon as he knows anything himself.'

It hadn't even occurred to her that she had used the Count's first name quite naturally, but Stefano noted it with a flick of one dark brow, though he said nothing for the moment. Either the Signora did not notice or was less concerned, for she was kind and gentle in her sympathy and would do nothing to embarrass her.

She was a very nice woman as well as a very attractive one, Jana thought, and if Giles did have to go into hospital for any length of time, she might well be glad of the Signora's presence. Stefano had mentioned that he and his mother would be staying for a matter of weeks, while the Count had said only a few days, but in the circumstances Jana could only hope that Stefano was right; it could make things rather difficult for her otherwise.

Being the only guest at the *palazzo* could lead to complications, she realised only too well, and she did not want to leave, not until Giles came back. She looked up when the Signora put down her cup and smiled across at her, although she was still very preoccupied with her own thoughts.

'You do not have your parents, Signorina Dennis? Only your uncle?'

'That's all.'

It occurred to Jana after a moment or two that she had been very off-hand when she replied to the kindly meant question, and she snatched her attention from listening for Marco and the doctor for a moment and smiled apologetically at Signora Abrizzi. 'I'm so sorry, *signora*, I wasn't paying attention—it was very rude of me. My parents died six years ago when I was sixteen and I've lived with Giles ever since.' She glanced once more at the partly open door, her eyes darkly anxious. 'He's been very good to me.'

'But of course you are concerned that he is ill, *mia cara signorina*, that is to be understood.' The fine dark eyes also switched to the half-open door and she smiled. 'I think I hear Marco coming now, so soon you will know how serious your uncle is ill, eh?'

There were voices; a murmured exchange for a few seconds and then a door closed and footsteps clipped smartly across the echoing tiles in the hall. A hand pushed the door wider and Jana was on her feet in a moment, looking across and not even giving him time to say anything before she got in her own short, apprehensive query.

'Marco?'

Once again her use of his first name was quite unconscious, she was concerned only with what news he had of her uncle, and he came straight across to her, taking her hands and looking down into her face while he spoke. 'It is as we feared, Jana. Giles has appendicitis and he must go into hospital.'

'Oh no!' Even though she had been expecting it, it still came as a shock to hear it confirmed, and she felt herself tremblingly anxious, despite the firm assurance of those enfolding hands.

'There is no need for undue alarm,' the Count assured her. 'He will be well taken care of, and he will be fit and well again before you know it, eh?'

'Yes. Yes, of course he will.' The strong hands still held hers tightly, and Jana tried to think clearly, to behave as if she was well able to cope with situations like this, when in fact she was neither used to emergencies nor confident enough to know what to do next. 'Thank you for letting me know, *signore*.'

The dark eyes studied her uncertain face for a second or two longer and then the Count shook his head. 'I have asked Giacomo to see to the packing of a *valigia* for him, so there is no need for you to trouble yourself about that, and he will be transported to the hospital as soon as possible.'

'I—I suppose I can go with him?'

She once again felt the need to consult him, as she had when she hovered in the doorway of her uncle's room while the doctor was there, and she found her own attitude of dependence hard to understand. She had never felt herself to be the dependent type before, and yet she seemed to be relying on Count Vincella quite a lot in this situation.

She would go with Giles, naturally, but she would feel so much better if someone else came too, and she was thinking specifically of the Count. She had never had much to do with hospitals, but she saw them as big, chillingly efficient places, and it was almost as if he knew how she felt, just as he had up there in her uncle's room.

'If you would like me to go with you, *piccina*, I will do so. Would you like me to?'

It was quite ridiculous to feel so relieved, but she made no pretence of how she felt, and the strong fingers that enclosed hers squeezed slightly, as if to encourage her to admit it. 'I'd be very grateful if you would, *signore*.' A glimpse of apology showed for a moment in her eyes when she looked up at him. 'I'm an awful coward about hospitals.'

'*Va bene!*' He released her fingers and turned to give his attention at last to his other guests, smiling across at Signora Abrizzi. 'I do not expect to be very long, Francesca, and when I return we will speak together about our plans, hah? In the meantime,' he gave Stefano a smile, 'I am sorry to deprive you of the company of the *signorina*, *mio caro* Stefano, but there will be other times when Jana is not so concerned with the health of her uncle!'

'*Sì.*'

Stefano's brief reply and the grudging concession he

conveyed with a shrug of his shoulders brought a brief upward tilt to Marco's black brows as he slid an unexpectedly familiar hand beneath Jana's arm. 'We will go and see your uncle now, Jana, hmm?'

An operation had been performed on Giles almost immediately, and the speed of his recovery was good so far, taking into account his age and a general lack of physical robustness that Jana had known nothing about until now. She had been so relieved to hear that he had come through the operation successfully and was recovering consciousness, that she had shed tears, and made no attempt to hide them.

That evening the Count had opened a bottle of special champagne and they had drunk to her uncle's speedy recovery. And as she held her glass high, in the toast to her uncle, her eyes had met Marco's for a moment only, but long enough to remind her of the moment when her nervousness of him had caused her to snap the stem of her glass and cut her fingers. He had smiled and inclined his head slightly when he caught her eye, so that she had the feeling that the toast was to her instead, and the Signora had flicked her dark gaze briefly from one to the other and smiled too.

After the operation, Jana's first visit to the hospital had been with the Count, but the next time she went Stefano Abrizzi had insisted on taking her, because, he said, he had more time on his hands than his cousin had. Which was probably true, Jana was ready to concede, although she felt sure her uncle would have liked to see Marco again.

Stefano was not fond of visiting the sick, however, especially someone he scarcely knew, and he had chafed at the boredom of two hours sitting in the hospital waiting room while Jana was in the ward. Apparently the experience was sufficient to discourage him, for the next morning he yielded the honour to his cousin once more, a gesture that Marco accepted with a slight smile, as if he knew quite well why it had been made.

Giles was evidently doing well, but it would be some time before he would be fit enough to undertake the arduous miles of walking that the project involved them in each day. The only alternative, as Jana saw it, was a return home to England until he was fully recovered, their work only partly completed. It was disappointing but at the moment she visualised no alternative, for they had been invited to the *palazzo* for the express purpose of working from it, and the idea of the Count entertaining them as purely visitors for probably several weeks did not even enter her head.

They had finished lunch, the Signora was spending the day with a friend and doing some shopping so there was only the three of them, when the Count said he would like to have a few words alone with Jana if it was convenient. She nodded, wondering what on earth made him think it would *not* be convenient, since she seldom went anywhere in case the hospital rang to say that Giles could come home. It was unlikely, she knew, but she firmly believed in the unexpected happening.

In the circumstances, Stefano had taken himself off somewhere in a mood, and Jana herself anticipated the conversation with foreboding, for what else could he have in mind but a return to England, with perhaps an open invitation for when her uncle was well again? She did not want to leave, she frankly admitted it in her own heart, and not simply because their work on the project was unfinished either. During the past week she had found herself acquiring a definite taste for living in the kind of luxury that the Palazzo Vincella provided, as well as for the enigmatic charm of their host.

With the prospect of leaving for home in mind, Jana watched the Count while he lit a cigarette, and hastily averted her gaze when he turned suddenly and caught her watching him. 'Is something wrong, Jana?' His voice could still cause her senses to respond, even after a week of living under his roof and hearing it every day—it fascinated her. 'Has Giles told you of my—our plan, perhaps?'

Shaking herself swiftly back to earth, Jana frowned at him curiously, wishing she could see his face more clearly instead of having it half-concealed by the smoke from his cigarette. 'Plan? What plan? Giles hasn't said anything to me, though I can guess what it will be.'

'Oh, you can?' He seated himself in an armchair opposite to the one she occupied and crossed his long legs, flicking an imaginary speck of ash from the knee of his slacks as he sometimes did. A nervous gesture was something Jana would never have expected of him, and yet she was rapidly reaching the conclusion that it was just that. 'Tell me, Jana, what do you think is our plan, eh? And what do you think of it?'

Jana made no pretence of not being sorry to leave, but she did not word it as frankly as she might have done if she had been speaking of it to anyone other than Count Vincella. 'I suppose it's the obvious thing if Giles is going to be some time before he's fit to carry on,' she told him, her reluctance to admit it quite plain in her voice as well as on her face. 'But I would have liked to stay longer, I have to admit.'

She thought he looked momentarily startled, but found it hard to believe, then he looked at her steadily for a moment through the smoke, with a suggestion of tightness about his mouth. 'So, *piccina*, you will not work with me, eh? You have already decided that you would rather go home to England than help me as you have helped your uncle—I am disappointed in you!'

Jana was staring at him hard, trying to make sense of what he was saying and finding it impossible with her mind in such chaos. She sat clasping her hands together tightly and there was a flush in her cheeks as she watched him warily, still not believing. 'You—I don't think I understand you, Count Vincella; I'm *sure* I don't understand you! You said——'

'I said that I am disappointed to learn you would prefer to leave rather than work on your uncle's project with me, Jana. That is what you have told me, is it not?'

Somewhere in the dark depths of his eyes, impatience showed, she thought, and shook her head again to clear it. It wasn't possible that he was talking of taking over Giles' project, and yet if she stopped to think about it, it was quite feasible. He was an historian, as Giles was. Without Giles' experience, it was true, but he was a very good amateur, Giles had said so, many times, and he knew Venice better than her uncle did; he could cover as much ground in less time with his knowledge, not to mention the privilege of his position.

Jana's hands rubbed together nervously for a moment, and she flicked the tip of her tongue over her lips, trying to grasp the situation and come to terms with it. 'You're saying that you've arranged to take over the project? Giles' project?'

'I am saying that Giles has agreed that I take over temporarily from him until he is fit to resume the work again,' Marco told her, and his dark eyes gleamed a challenge at her through the concealing smoke screen. 'I admit that I was very pleased to do so, but then I anticipated having your invaluable assistance, just as Giles had; I did not anticipate that you would refuse it to me.'

'Oh, but I didn't!' He held her gaze steadily, and she knew he had never been in any doubt about her co-operation at all, no matter how he had tangled her in his maze of misunderstanding. 'I didn't know,' she insisted. 'I'd no idea that Giles had arranged for you to take on his side of it. I knew it was going to be some time before he was able to do anything more about it himself, but I thought—I mean, I anticipated us both going home until he was fit again.'

A slight smile hovered about that firm mouth for a moment, and the dark eyes were once more challenging her to explain her meaning. 'And you thought that I would not have my old friend here unless he was working on his book, *piccina*? You believed that I would see him go all the way back to England rather than give him time to recover, when he is sick and weak from hospital?' He shook his head slowly, as if her judgment of him had indeed been as harsh as he depicted it, and had it not been for that glimmer of amusement that mocked her from the depth of his eyes, she would have believed he took it to heart. 'You do not have a very good opinion of me, I fear, Jana.'

'You know me better than that too!' Jana retorted swiftly, her colour high as she hastily avoided his eyes. 'I don't see you as some kind of medieval monster, *signore*, and you know it! You've been very good while Giles is in hospital and I don't know what I'd have done without your help when he was taken ill.'

That steady gaze from the facing chair was disconcerting, especially when she thought of herself working as closely with him during the next week or two as she had with Giles. She had been frank about her dependency on him during Giles' illness, and he was still taking stock of her opinion, if his expression was any guide.

'I have noticed that you call your uncle by his christian name,' he observed after a moment or two, and Jana blinked at him in surprise.

'I always have, ever since I was old enough to be thought of as a grown-up. Ever since Giles took me under his wing when my parents died.'

A smile hovered about his mouth and showed, warmly dark, in his eyes as he leaned forward to press out the cigarette in an ashtray. 'Then since you are to come under my wing, for a while at least, *piccina*, will you not afford me the same privilege?'

Jana remembered calling him by his first name, once or twice, she thought, when Giles was first ill and she did not stop to think of such things. He had accepted it quite naturally, as naturally as she had used it, and she did not know why she had since reverted to calling him the more formal *signore*. She looked at him through the thick silkiness of her lashes, then nodded her head.

'Yes, of course, if you prefer it,' she said. 'I didn't know——'

'If I would prefer to be kept at a distance by the formality of *signore*?' he suggested soft-voiced, and Jana shook her head instinctively.

'No, of course not!'

He leaned back in his chair and regarded her for a moment with a hint of smile on his mouth and that slightly mocking look in his eyes that was one of the first things she remembered noticing about him. 'Then if we are to work closely together, Jana, you will remember to use my name, eh?'

It was in response to that glint of mockery that she lifted her chin slightly and met his eyes for a moment. 'Yes, of course, Marco; I'll treat you exactly as I would Giles, as you're taking his place.'

He narrowed his eyes slightly for a moment, then laughed, and she thought the words he said in Italian were a curse, she was not sure, but he was still laughing when Stefano came in to join them.

CHAPTER THREE

IT did not take Jana very long to discover that working with Marco was much more demanding than doing the same thing with Giles. For one thing he set a much faster pace which she was more or less obliged to keep up with or else protest, and that was something she was loath to do in the circumstances. She was not at all sure just how inconvenient he found it, taking on her uncle's task, so complaining about the way he went about it seemed ungracious to say the least.

With Giles she had been able to take her time occasionally, and linger sometimes to admire places and things that were not directly concerned with the period they were dealing with. Marco, on the other hand, seemed to be trying to cram in as much as possible in the shortest possible time, and she could only think it would be because he had other things to do.

He did not practise his profession as an architect, but he must have filled his days with some activity before she and her uncle arrived, and taking over from her uncle must have caused some disturbance in his way of life. With this in mind Jana had kept up with his enthusiastic pace for some days now, but with the sun so hot and being required to cover so much ground, she just had to call a halt.

Her notebook was filled with her untidy shorthand, as well as several professionally skilful sketches contributed by Marco, which she could not help but envy, and she wondered if he really believed that her uncle had worked at the same killing pace. She kept up with him as they emerged from the blessed coolness of a narrow passageway into

Campiello Querini-Stampalia, but then she deliberately slowed her step until it became so noticeable that Marco turned and frowned at her curiously, and eventually she stopped altogether.

She stood at the corner of a bridge that spanned a narrow canal and looked down at the water lapping softly and the spangled lights that danced under the curved stone, where the sun struck the surface, and she knew he was watching her. She hadn't wanted to object, but she felt she had gone as far as she could for one morning, and whether or not it appeared ungracious, she had to call a halt; at least for the time being.

'Something is wrong, Jana?'

He was stood close beside her so that she could sense the slight tension of his curiosity physically, and she wondered if he had any idea how far he had walked her that morning. Her expression showed a hint of the rebellion she felt, in the down-drawn softness of her mouth and in her eyes which she kept hidden from him for the moment.

'I'm tired, that's all,' she declared firmly and with a trace of defiance because she still wasn't happy about complaining. 'I'm tired of walking so far and so fast and I need a break, Marco. I've walked over half Venice this morning!'

'Not quite, *piccina*!'

She did not look up, but her mouth pursed slightly in reproach. 'Don't you ever get tired?'

'Not very often.' It was difficult to judge his exact reaction to her protest, but he answered her with apparent willingness, even though one black brow was arched, suggesting he was puzzled by her sudden revolt. 'Like most Venetians, I am accustomed to walking quite a lot.'

'I thought most Venetians used the *vaporetti* or the *diretto*——'

'Ah, you have learned the Venetian's name for the quicker service, eh?'

The fact seemed to surprise him for some reason, and his response had the effect of distracting her from her complaint for a moment; but only for a moment, then she once more looked away. 'Giles and I occasionally used it, but I thought *you* usually used your own motor-launch!'

She was being petty, Jana knew it, and very ungracious in the circumstances, but she blamed her mood on her aching feet and the fact that the sun seemed never to have been hotter. It would have salved her conscience to some extent, she admitted, if he had waxed indignant and pointed out that he was giving a great deal of his time to her uncle's project, but instead he was quiet and evidently trying to understand, as he watched her steadily.

'Very occasionally I use the *motoscafo*, but I also frequently walk!' The tone of his voice suggested he was becoming impatient and she did not want him losing his patience with her in the circumstances.

Nevertheless she could not keep up the pace he had set so far and she had to tell him so before they went any further. Resting both arms along the cool stone parapet, she gazed down into the water. 'I walked for hours with Giles during those first three days,' she told him, 'but it isn't the same with you, Marco—you walk so much faster than Giles and I can't always keep up with you, and it's hot——'

'I am sorry!'

She hadn't meant him to apologise, and she shook her head quickly to deny the need for it. 'Oh, I don't suppose you realised,' she allowed hastily. 'But you have a much longer stride and also you're not used to having me along.' An upward glance revealed an unexpected hint of warmth in his eyes that made her take the first step towards surrender. 'Where are we going next?'

Marco indicated a building on the opposite side of the canal. 'Just across to the other side of the *rio*, to the Palazzo Querini, do you know it?' Jana nodded. 'There are some very good examples of Renaissance paintings in the collection there, and I am sure Giles would wish them to be included.' Dark eyes took note of the set of her mouth and the lingering traces of that slightly rebellious pout, and he shook his head. 'First we will go and take notes of them, Jana, and then you shall sit down and have lunch, you have my word!'

His eyes as well as that irresistible voice sought to persuade her and, despite her tiredness, Jana knew she was going to be persuaded; it was inevitable; so she prepared to yield without yet admitting it. 'Will it take very long?' The thought of lunch was very attractive and she thought the building he had indicated looked much too big for a tour of its treasures to be accomplished in a few minutes. 'It looks enormous, Marco, and I'm really serious about taking time off. I'm so tired I could——'

'Please do not threaten me with anything too dramatic, Jana, there is no need! It will possibly take twenty minutes for us to make our notes, and then I will take you to lunch at a restaurant I know, one you will not know but will enjoy, I think—that is my promise. You will trust me to keep my promise, hah?'

It was fairly quiet in the little square, away from the busier tourist places, and for a few moments Jana felt strangely isolated from the rest of the world. The long brown fingers that were laid lightly on her arm, and the blatant persuasion of those dark eyes, were all that existed for her for several minutes while she thought over what he had said. Something, she thought, was not quite clear in her mind, and she wanted to be sure.

'Did you say that you'd give me lunch at a restaurant?' she asked, and scarcely noticed the slight huskiness in her voice.

Marco nodded, guiding her away from the parapet and on over the bridge in the direction of the Palazzo Querini, the way he wanted her to go. 'Surely you will not refuse to have lunch with me?' he asked, and his finger-tips touched lightly on her flesh. 'Will you, Jana?'

'Oh no! No, of course I won't.' In some curious way she felt less tired suddenly, and wondered if the hand so lightly guiding her could possibly have such an effect on her. There was something very encouraging about the long brown fingers that curved lightly into her flesh, persuading her along beside him, and after a moment Jana looked up at him and smiled. 'I haven't lunched out for ages!' she told him, and wondered why he smiled the way he did.

The entrance hall of the Palazzo Querini was stuccoed and brightly painted, but in view of her protestations about being tired, Marco bypassed the rest of the numerous rooms full of art treasures that covered almost every period of Venetian history, and led her directly to Room IX which, he informed her, was devoted entirely to Renaissance art, the period they were concerned with.

Presented with such a treasure house, most of Jana's earlier tiredness vanished as she noted and admired, directed by Marco's quiet, pedantic instructions, selecting and choosing from the treasury that which he thought would most appeal to his old friend. It was a labour of love, that much was obvious, and somehow his devotion to his city's treasures always inspired her, no matter how hard he tried her physically.

'The Bellini Virgin and Child.' Jana jotted it down obediently with appropriate notes on colours and details and so on, following him about the room which they had to themselves for the moment. 'And certainly the Palma Vecchio portraits, do you not think, Jana?'

The work of the elder Palma was known to her, but she had never before seen these portraits; obviously a pair and unfinished in fact, but breathtaking for all that. The female

portrait especially appealed to Jana, with its gentle browns
and yellows, and the shy, wistful expression of the sitter
that was still hauntingly touching even after four and a half
centuries.

'She's lovely.'

She caught Marco's eye immediately after she passed her
opinion and saw the way he smiled. 'You know who she is?'
She shook her head, something in that smile making her
feel slightly lightheaded suddenly. 'She was Paola Pruili,
the bride of Francesco Querini. It was painted, like the one
of her husband, to celebrate their marriage in about 1528.
You find her very lovely?'

'Don't you?' Jana kept her eyes on the portrait because
she found it incredibly hard to look directly at him. 'All
that time and she's still lovely.'

'But of course!' Marco gave the picture a brief glance,
then returned his gaze to Jana's slightly flushed face and
the fringe of thick lashes that hid her eyes from him. He
slid a long finger beneath her chin and raised her face to
him while he gazed down at the tremulous softness of her
mouth for a moment, a hint of a smile on his lips. 'All
beautiful women should be painted at the peak of their
beauty, for in that way men can enjoy them for much
longer, hmm?' The effect of his voice sent a shivering sensation all through her body until she felt herself trembling.
'Perhaps one day someone as talented as Palma will paint a
portrait of you, Jana, sì?'

The room was empty except for the two of them, but
somehow Jana felt all those painted eyes watching from
their gilded frames. Autocratic, shy or frankly sensual, they
all seemed to be concentrated on the two living intruders
into their Renaissance grandeur, and after a second or two
Jana moved her head very slightly so that she was free of
the supporting finger.

'If anyone did,' she said in a breathlessly husky voice, 'I

wouldn't have anywhere to hang it. I haven't a *palazzo*, and nothing less would be suitable for a Palma, or someone like him.'

Briefly and startlingly Marco's lips brushed her mouth, the pressure of his body arousing a stunning reaction from her senses. 'I have,' he said softly, and took the notebook from her nerveless fingers, closing it carefully before handing it back to her. 'Will you have that lunch that I promised you now?'

The restaurant that Marco had been so sure she would enjoy was without a doubt the most attractive one Jana had seen anywhere, although her knowledge of Venetian restaurants was limited since she and Giles had never done more than have coffee during their long sessions of exploration. They had always returned to the Palazzo Vincella for lunch and dinner.

It seemed like walking into another world when they left a narrow *rughetta* with houses both sides and passed through a passageway into the sun again. A winding stone staircase led them upwards from the *fondamenta* to a paved terrace set out with tables and edged around with wrought iron scrolls, overlooking one of the smaller canals. Trellises draped with vines and hung with potted plants made each table a small private rendezvous of its own, and cast intriguing shadow patterns across the occupants.

The view across the water was one so familiar from all quarters of Venice; one of elegant but faded façades and reflected roof-tops soaring into spires and cupolas to the soft shimmer of a Venetian sky. The buildings appearing to rise straight from the water without even the support of the *fondamente* on which they were built. It was enchanting, and Jana's artless pleasure evidently amused Marco, for he smiled in that slightly mocking way that was now familiar but vaguely disturbing.

'You find it to your liking?' he asked as they took their places at one of the small, intimately private tables, and Jana nodded agreement.

'It's lovely; so—romantic.' She hesitated to use the word in view of that slight air of mockery about him, but it was the most suitable one she could think of and she refused to be deterred. 'And I imagine not many people know it's here, do they?'

Marco sat facing her with the little table between them making only a flimsy barrier, and she was made stunningly aware of the physical magnetism of him as he leaned forward slightly, resting his elbows on the table top. For a moment or two his dark eyes studied her in a way that made it difficult for her to think clearly, then he smiled and turned to take the menu from a tall, solemn-faced man who was apparently the proprietor.

'If you refer to visitors to Venice, *piccina*, you are correct in assuming that they seldom discover this place, but it is very popular with Venetians.' He glanced up at the man waiting deferentially beside him, and smiled. 'Is that not so, Lucio?'

The man inclined his dark head solemnly and accepted the fact with aplomb. '*Sì, ha ragione, signore.*'

Jana made no secret of her appreciation, and she smiled, not only at the view but at the pleasantness of her immediate surroundings too. The building itself was obviously old, as so much of Venice seemed to be, its ornate façade suggesting that at one time it had been a small *palazzo*, and its first floor balcony decked round with trellis and smothered in flowering vines offered the most enchanting setting in which to enjoy good food and wine. Music reached them from somewhere nearby, but did not intrude into conversation, and there was sufficient shade to make sitting out pleasurable without completely obscuring the sun.

'It's really lovely!' She endorsed her first impression

unhesitatingly and the man once more inclined his head in grave acceptance.

'*Tante grazie, signorina.*'

When she looked across at Marco, there was a hint of mischief in her eyes. 'Now that I know where it is, I can find my way here again—even if I'm not a Venetian!'

'Do you know where it is, *piccina*?' Marco's dark eyes gently mocked her certainty. 'Could you find your way here again, do you think—without my help?'

Jana was not sure what she had expected him to answer, she had not even stopped to consider what she meant by it, but it would have been in keeping, she thought, if he had made some equally superficial remark about bringing her again himself in the future. Instead he had given her the impression that if she came again she would have to do so without his guidance, and she felt curiously let down for a moment. It was that sensation that made her respond as she did.

'I could try!'

Marco did not comment, but bent his head to study the menu once more, and after a few seconds he offered her the double-paged list, held open between his long fingers. 'Will you choose for yourself, Jana, or will you allow me to choose for you?'

It was clear which he would prefer, and Jana was quite happy to let him choose, so she shook her head and made no attempt to take the menu from him. 'You choose, please,' she told him. 'My Italian isn't up to reading menus and you might lose patience if I go all the way through it asking for translations.'

He needed no second bidding, and when the meal came Jana could find no fault at all with his choice, he had judged her taste perfectly. *Zucchini ripieni*, to start with, arrived as stuffed baby marrows and were delicious, and in deference to the heat of the day a favourite summer dish followed, consisting of very thinly sliced roast veal served in a coating of creamy sauce that tasted faintly of something Jana could not identify until Marco told her it was anchovy. Finishing with tiny wild strawberries and sweet, golden Frascati wine from the Rome district, she felt she had been thoroughly spoiled and made no secret of the fact that she revelled in the sensation.

They had been a long time over lunch, but Marco, in contrast to his earlier sense of urgency, seemed to be in no hurry to leave as he sat enjoying the silky golden wine with a sensuous kind of pleasure that affected Jana curiously. His eyes were more languorous and a half smile hovered about his mouth as he regarded her from the thick shadow of his lashes without speaking for several minutes.

'You have enjoyed your meal?'

There was only one possible answer, and Jana gave it unhesitatingly. 'It was the most wonderful meal I've ever had—I can honestly say that I've never tasted anything so good!'

Her obvious enthusiasm pleased him, that much was clear, but somehow she suspected that somewhere too lurked a hint of amusement in those dark eyes for her almost naïve response. Then his gaze strayed for a moment to the buildings along the opposite side of the canal and she wondered, briefly, if Venetians themselves ever tired of the endless sense of history that surrounded them on every side, and the incredible treasurehouse of ancient buildings and art treasures. Venice was unique and she found it enchanting, as did millions of others, but she had not lived there all her life as Marco had.

'You love your city, don't you, Marco?'

She spoke softly and on impulse, for it was due in part to the wine having smoothed away certain inhibitions that she asked the question at all. But he gave her his attention once more, smiling slightly behind the wine glass he held in long brown fingers that seemed to caress the slender stem lovingly.

'Do you not also love Venice?' he challenged, but gave her no time to reply. 'But of course I love my city, *piccina*, all Venetians do; is it not natural that we should?'

'Yes, of course it is.'

She was momentarily at a loss, something in his voice and the dark depth of his eyes robbing her of her normal confidence. Then she looked across the water once more and imagined how heaven-sent it would be to be born an artist in the midst of so much richness and inspiration. But she was brought back swiftly by a hand that gently covered her own as it lay on the table, long brown fingers lightly curled, just enough to take her attention from the scene across the water and the visions of being an inspired artist.

'That is why I grieve for the fate of our city if something is not done to preserve it, Jana.'

Jana was as fully aware of the plight of Venice and the uncertainty of her future as most of the rest of the world, and it appalled her to think of this beautiful though slightly faded city slowly sinking back into the water from which it had risen more than fifteen centuries ago. It must be an even harder prospect to face for Venetians, like Marco, and for the first time Jana understood a little of the enormity of the loss it would be to the people of this very special place.

'It would be an enormous job—an almost impossible job, Marco, I can't imagine how they can even go about starting it; it's just too vast to contemplate.'

'But somehow it must be done, and done before the damage is irreparable!'

There was passion in the depth of his voice that she had never heard before, and the long fingers that clasped her hand had an almost cruel strength, as if by impressing his physical strength on her he could better impress her with the urgency of his concern. Jana did nothing to try and relieve the pressure, but watched the expressions on that dark and infinitely changeable face as he sat in the shadows, the shimmering reflections of the water below darting across a wide sensual mouth and thick dark lashes that cast black shadows on high smooth cheekbones.

She looked down at their clasped hands, wanting to say something constructive but unable to find the words. 'Something is being done, isn't it, Marco?' She had the dark eyes on her again, steady and serious, judging the depth of her feeling and matching it with his own. 'I remember before we left home there were funds being raised and appeals, to save all the millions of treasures there are here.'

He nodded and a shrug heaved his broad shoulders almost resignedly. 'There are so many people concerned, practical in their concern, it is very heartwarming, but it will take so much and we must work so quickly. That is why——' He shifted his gaze from her face suddenly and looked down at their hands clasped together on the table, hesitating, seeking for words it seemed, and yet she found that hard to believe of someone as fluent as he normally was. 'That is why I am contemplating taking a step that to me—to my whole family—is irrevocable.'

'You're not leaving Venice, Marco?' She could not have said why the idea distressed her so much, but Marco was shaking his head slowly and she almost heaved a sigh of relief.

'No, no, Jana; the Vincellas will not leave Venice until Venice is no longer here for us, and I pray that day will never come. But there are things that we must do, or at least consider doing, which need such careful thought.'

Jana had the feeling that in some curious way she had come closer to him in these few minutes than she ever had

before, and she responded to the realisation impulsively.
Placing her other hand over the one that held hers, she
smoothed her finger-tips over the tanned skin gently while
she briefly held his eyes.

'If there's something you need to talk about to someone,
Marco, I'm ready to listen.' A small half-smile ventured to
ease the dark seriousness of his mood. 'Giles tells me that
I'm a very good listener.'

Marco did nothing for a moment, and his silence pro-
voked a flutter of apprehension in her, for she feared she
might have embarrassed him; but in the same second that
she started to withdraw her hand, he looked across at her
and smiled. Taking both her hands in his, he turned them
over and pressed his lips to the soft warmth of her palms
before folding them together and clasping them tightly.

'I am quite sure that you are, *piccina*, but you are very
young to be troubled with the problems of others.'

'Oh, I don't mind in the least if it will help!' She looked
at him earnestly and her heart fluttered in disturbing response to the strong pressure of his hands. 'And I wish you
wouldn't take your role as Giles' stand-in quite so literally,
Marco. I'm not a little girl, you know, despite that very
pretty Italian version that you call me.' She caught his eye
briefly and coloured. 'I asked Signora Abrizzi what *piccina*
meant,' she confessed, 'and she told me it was something
like "little girl".'

The hard fingers pressed more tightly for a second and a
dark brow questioned her reaction. 'And you do not like it
that I call you *piccina*?'

Determinedly matter-of-fact, Jana shook her head. 'I
don't mind it in the least as long as you don't mean it
literally.' She hurried on when she thought she detected the
smallest of frowns threatening those black brows. 'But I'll
understand if you don't want to tell me what's on your

mind, Marco. You'd probably much rather talk to Giles about it when he's better—after all, you've been friends for some time, and I know——'

'You know little, *piccina*, if you think I am refusing to confide in you!' He shook his head and smiled at her, though it did nothing, she noticed, to brighten the seriousness of his eyes. He let go her hands suddenly and refilled both their glasses with the last of the cool golden Frascati. 'But I did not give you lunch in order that I might unburden my problems on to your young shoulders, Jana. Since you encourage me, however——' He raised his glass to her and drank deeply from it before placing it back carefully on the table in front of him.

'Sometimes if you talk about a thing——' she ventured, and Marco nodded slowly.

'*Sì, sì, piccina*, I know!'

He was close to confiding in her, Jana knew it, and she probed gently but insistently towards his confidence. 'Have the Vincella family always been here?'

'For a little more than three hundred years.' A brief sardonic smile questioned her opinion. 'Is that always, Jana, would you say?'

'It's a very long time!'

'*Sì*, it is a very long time. I think that now we are Venetians, eh?' Jana nodded without speaking, encouraging him to go on. 'You know of the Eagle of the Vincella?'

Jana frowned curiously, remembering the huge stone replica of an eagle that loomed so menacingly from the façade of the *palazzo*, above the almost obliterated coat-of-arms. Wings spread and carrying a man in its enormous talons, it had never yet failed to bring a responsive shudder from her, as it did now.

'I've seen the big carved eagle that juts out above the portico,' she told him. 'It's part of your coat-of-arms, isn't it? I've always assumed it was as it's up there above the portico.'

Marco nodded. 'Giles has not told you of the history of the Vincella?'

He seemed surprised, but Jana pulled a face and smiled as she shook her head. 'You know how single-minded Giles is. He's concerned with the Renaissance at the moment, and the *palazzo* is later, isn't it?'

'Only a little later,' Marco agreed, but followed her meaning well enough, for he knew his old friend's purposeful adherence to his current interest. 'I understand your meaning, however. Giles would not consider it of interest to your present project and so he would not mention it. The Palazzo Vincella was built in the period of baroque, it is too late for Renaissance.'

'Exactly!' She drank from her glass and looked at him hopefully, her eyes questioning. 'Is it something about that stone eagle that's bothering you at the moment, Marco?'

'No, not the stone eagle, *piccina*. There is another, much more valuable one, though the one you speak of is a replica of it. Perhaps you do not know either that the Vincella family fortunes were laid in the seventeenth century, in a little town a long way from here. In those days the family were very minor land-owners, not *aristocrazia*, you understand; they lived in hill country in the south by a small town called Vincella. They were very devout people and, while they would probably not have been above relieving some unwary *nobile* of some of his treasure, the treasures of the church were sacred to them and they would never have touched them for any reason. So—when the head of the family and some of his sons came upon a gang of robbers looting riches destined for the Papal treasury in Rome, they fought them off fiercely and put them to flight.'

'The robbers being symbolised by the man the eagle has in its talons,' Jana guessed, and he nodded.

'That is right. Two of his four sons were lost in the fight, but the Papal treasure was sent safely on its way once more. The matter was reported to Pope Innocent the Eleventh when he received the gifts, and for his service to the church, Gaspare Fabriano was handsomely rewarded—a title, Conte di Vincella, and some land, as well as the eagle. He and his sons, it was said, had pounced like eagles upon the would-be desecrators of holy property and therefore it was fitting that part of their reward should take a similar form.'

'The Eagle of the Vincella!'

Marco nodded, but his eyes had a look that betrayed his momentary absence from the world of today, as if he could see in his mind's eye that ancient battle taking place and the rich reward it had brought his family. 'It is made of solid gold and its eyes are perfect topaz set in circles of rubies and diamonds.'

Jana's imagination could not cope with such a fabulous creature, and she stared at him curiously. 'It's here? In Venice?'

'It is in the *palazzo*, hidden away and seldom even looked at. A mythical creature, beautiful but pointless in an age such as we live in—out of its time, rather like our lovely city. Its present day value is something in the region of two million lire, or a quarter of a million American dollars.'

Jana stared at him for a moment, too stunned to say anything, then she moistened her lips with the tip of her tongue and tried to imagine the existence of such a creature. 'That's something like—a hundred and twenty, or a hundred and twenty-five thousand pounds,' she said huskily, and Marco looked at her and smiled wryly.

'A useful contribution to the restoration of Venice, eh, *piccina*?'

'Oh no, Marco, you couldn't!'

Shock made her breathless and she was shaking her head

urgently, as if it was herself that he was threatening to deprive of her greatest treasure. What he said was true, she could see that, and she could to some extent understand his desire to make some massive contribution to the restoration of his beloved city, but she could not even begin to understand how he could think of parting with the symbol of his family's honour—something they had held in trust for over three hundred years.

'You won't, will you, Marco?'

It was as if she pleaded on her own behalf, and she saw the way the dark brows flicked upwards in question. 'You do not approve of such a contribution?'

It was nothing at all to do with what she thought or felt about it, Jana knew, and she would probably have done much better to simply declare herself in no position to pass an opinion, but somehow she could not remain aloof from it. She toyed with the stem of her glass to give her hands something to do, and did not look at him for the moment while she tried to get him to see how wrong it would be to let the Eagle go after all this time.

'I just don't see how you can bring yourself to even think about giving it away——'

'Not to give it away, *piccina*—it is worth one quarter of a million dollars!'

'But to let it go out of the family after so long; out of the country most likely——'

'Very likely, I imagine! There are many Italians in America, surely one would pay one quarter of a million American dollars for such a treasure from the old country!'

'Oh, how can you treat it so—so cold-bloodedly?' She was becoming rash in her anxiety to convince him. 'Doesn't it mean anything to you? Your family's most precious possession to be sold to the highest bidder—and what about when *you* have sons and they inherit? Will they thank you for selling their inheritance?'

There was a slightly ominous look about the dark face that should have warned her, Jana supposed, but she was too carried away in her determination to convince him that Gaspare Fabriano's hard-earned reward should not be sold to someone who would remove it from its native soil that she did not much care if he grew angry or not; and he was undoubtedly growing angry, it showed in the glittering darkness of his eyes.

'I have no sons to consider, Jana, and I cannot think that Stefano is so filled with family feeling that he will treat the matter half so seriously as you seem to be doing!'

'Stefano?'

He looked briefly impatient, then shook his head while he explained. 'Stefano is the next in line unless I marry and have a family.'

'And suppose you *do* marry?'

The almost black eyes held hers with piercing intensity, like chips of jet between those thick lashes. 'Suppose that I do marry, *ragazza*? Do you suppose that my bride will have married me simply because I have the Eagle of Vincella? The trinket is mine while I live and I may do with it as I please!'

'Of *course, signore*!'

The silence between them was so complete that not even the warm comforting sounds from the adjacent trellised alcoves intruded into it. And Jana felt a small cold feeling of regret in the pit of her stomach as she sat with her hands rolled tightly together, looking down at the table top rather than at the sternly handsome face opposite.

She had never seen him angry before, and she found him rather awesome in his anger, for there was a suggestion of suppressed violence about him that evoked a certain excitement as well as apprehension. The Eagle was his, as Marco said, it was his to do with as he pleased. She would never understand his apparent preparedness to part with it, but she had to admit his right to do so if he wanted to. She had to be the one to apologise, there was no doubt about that, and she glanced briefly at him through her lashes as she passed the tip of her tongue anxiously across her lips.

'I'm sorry, Marco.'

He said nothing for several seconds until she began to fear that she had really offended him, but then he looked up at last and she could see the trace of regret in his eyes too, and took heart from it. He shook his head and after a moment his mouth eased into a half smile.

'No, no, *piccola*! By telling you the story of the Eagle and what I am trying to decide to do about it, I invited your comment, therefore I cannot object when you do so with such fervour!'

'I don't have the right to object at all, it's yours to sell or not, as you decide.'

'*Sì.*' He picked up his almost empty glass and drained the very last drops of wine from it, then sat and twirled the slender stem in his long fingers for a moment. 'I still have to decide what I will do and I could wish that it could be decided without so much——'

'So much heart-searching?' Jana suggested softly, and he smiled again faintly as he shook his head.

'I have much need to search my heart, *piccina*, for I have to decide which is the more worthy of two causes, and it is not easy; it is not easy at all.' He was talking, Jana realised, more from the need to talk than from any special desire to confide in her particularly, and the idea of him having such a need surprised her momentarily. He held her gaze for a moment, his eyes darkly serious, but then he laughed and shook his head suddenly, touching her hand with his finger-tips, lightly and provocatively, so that her senses responded to the unexpected touch of him as they were bound to. 'But we grow gloomy, eh, Jana? This is not the mood of Venice, and there are happier ways of raising lire—we have plans for that too!'

'To raise funds?' She almost regretted the reappearance of that faintly mocking smile, although it lightened his mood, and she looked at him curiously. 'What ideas do you have, Marco?'

'It is a plan of Francesca's, although we have the need to—co-operate?—together if she must have the use of the Palazzo Vincella to make it possible!'

'Something exciting?'

The dark eyes smiled at her mockingly. 'I have no doubt that you will think so, *piccina*, for I think that you are a *romantica*, eh?'

'Perhaps.' Jana admitted it a little uneasily, but it did not stem her curiosity.

'So also is Francesca,' said Marco, convinced he was right in both instances. 'You know that Francesca is the widow of Emilio Abrizzi, the industrialist?' She hadn't known, but she could well believe that his cousin was the widow of a millionaire, everything about her pointed to immense wealth; she nodded. 'She and Stefano between them know most of the wealthiest people in Europe and America, and Francesca plans to have them gathered all together under our roof!'

Jana stared at him blankly at first, unable to grasp the immensity of the idea, then she shook her head slowly. 'A—a kind of party? To raise funds? Oh, but, Marco, that's marvellous, it could raise thousands!'

Marco was laughing, mocking her wonder at the prospect, and shaking his head. 'Hundreds of thousands, *piccina*, perhaps more than two million lire!'

'So you won't have to sell the Vincella Eagle!'

A swift shake of his head dismissed that subject, and he

watched her with bold bright eyes, still amused by her excitement. 'That excites you, Jana? A costume ball at the *palazzo*, with so many people it will seem no bigger than a wooden hut! Will you like that?'

Jana's eyes darted over his face searchingly, her smile almost vanished as she faced an entirely new prospect. A gathering such as Marco mentioned was right outside her scope and she could not see herself as part of it. The fact that Marco obviously did both surprised and startled her. Briefly the tip of her tongue appeared and moistened her lips and she frowned at him uncertainly.

'Shall I be going?'

'Will you not?' he countered, his quiet voice mocking her surprise. 'You and Giles are my friends, why should you not be there also? Of course you will be there, Jana!'

'But——' She shook her head, unable to visualise herself at such an event, but at the same time excited at the idea of going. Then she laughed, a small tremblingly uncertain laugh as she shook her head. 'I've never been to anything more grand than a local dance with a boy-friend,' she told him. 'I'm not sure I can move into international society that easily, Marco.'

'You will not refuse to go?' When she looked up at him again she saw that now all too familiar gleam of mockery in his eyes and he leaned forward slightly in his chair, lowering his voice to suit the suggestion of confidence between them. 'If you do not care for the feelings of Francesca and myself,' he said, 'you would not wish for Stefano to be disappointed, would you, *piccina*?'

It was curious, Jana thought, and rather annoying, how she niggled with dislike whenever he suggested there was some reason she should be willing to do as Stefano wanted, simply because he saw her as irresistibly attracted to his good-looking young cousin. It was quite unconscious when she lifted her chin as she answered him. 'Oh no,' she said after a moment, 'I'd hate to disappoint Stefano!'

Marco's dark brows noted the edge on her voice and questioned it for a second before he smiled and squeezed her fingers, then called for their bill. *'Bene!'* he said approvingly.

CHAPTER FOUR

THE most exciting thing to happen during the next week or so was Giles' discharge from hospital, although Jana as well as her uncle realised that it would be some time before he could resume the same active role he had before. He now spent most of his time resting but at the same time going through the copious notes that Jana had typed out for him, covering the research that she and Marco had done during his absence.

She and Marco continued with their daily expeditions, although once or twice when they set off on another day's research, Jana felt a twinge of conscience about leaving her uncle behind, partly, although it did not make sense, because she found it hard to disguise the fact that she enjoyed working with Marco so much.

She did not delude herself for a moment that their relationship had altered in any way, but since their lunch together he had relaxed his punishing programme to allow her to take things a little more easily. He seemed to have less desire to rush around from one place to another as if his one wish was to complete the project as quickly as possible.

As far as Giles himself was concerned, he seemed not at all averse to playing a more sedentary role, and spent the days quite happily poring over the material they collected for him, discussing it with Marco or checking facts from a pile of books that Marco provided him with. Taking into consideration his usual reticence with strangers, it had surprised Jana to notice how quickly he and the Signora became friendly. A couple of times when she and Marco had returned, she had gone in search of him and found him with Signora Abrizzi, checking notes and conversing quite animatedly together.

He had been back from the hospital a little over a week when Jana was reminded of the Vincella Eagle; something in the notes they were going through reminded her of the legend and she remembered how surprised Marco had been that Giles had not already told her the story. She had hoped, after being told that it was actually lodged in the *palazzo* somewhere, that she might be allowed a glimpse of it, but nothing more had been said about it so far.

When she raised the subject with Giles he frowned. 'It's a magnificent piece of workmanship, my dear, but I'm afraid it's a subject that Marco and I don't see eye to eye about.'

Surprised, Jana blinked at him curiously. 'You mean you don't think it's as valuable as Marco says it is?'

'Oh no, my dear, it has nothing to do with its value; I have no doubt at all that it would fetch an enormous sum if it was ever to be put on the open market——'

'About two million lire, Marco estimates.'

Giles pursed his lips in a silent whistle. 'Then he is probably right. But no, our difference of opinion is over the age of the thing; Marco claims that it was given to his family in the late seventeenth century by Innocent the Eleventh, and I have no doubt he is right about that too. But whereas he classes it as Renaissance, I insist that it is too florid and ostentatious, as well as too late to qualify—to my mind the creature is definitely baroque.'

'Oh, I see, it's a matter of dates!'

She smiled to herself, but Giles was quite serious about it. 'Marco claims, reasonably enough I suppose, that it would have been produced at a much earlier date than the time it came into the Vincella family, and that therefore it qualifies as a Renaissance piece. But this is an instance when I have to disagree with him, I'm afraid, the Eagle is very definitely baroque; made in the period when the two styles were overlapping, no doubt, but not pure Renaissance.'

Which was the reason Giles had not mentioned it to her, Jana suspected, and smiled wryly to herself. It was so seldom that her uncle and Marco did not see eye to eye that he did not like to mention matters on which they did not agree. But her curiosity about the Eagle of the Vincella was increased rather than diminished by the controversy, and she wished there was some way of her getting a sight of it.

'Would he show it to me, do you suppose?' she asked, looking down at her notes rather than at her uncle, and Giles looked vaguely surprised for a moment.

'Possibly, my dear. Why don't you ask him?'

That was a drawback, as Jana saw it, for if Marco was of a mind for her to see the controversial Eagle he would surely have shown it to her by now, having told her of its existence. She shuffled the notes she had in her hand and shrugged. 'I don't know—I just don't want him to think I'm too inquisitive.'

'Oh, but I'm quite sure he wouldn't think that, Jana, why should he?'

Again she shrugged uneasily and shook her head. 'Did you know he was thinking of selling it?'

She realised only when she saw the look of stunned surprise on Giles' face that she should have been more tactful about asking even her uncle that question. Marco had told her in confidence, she felt sure, and she had the feeling that she had been the first one to be taken into his confidence about the possible fate of the Eagle. It wasn't easy to say why, but she had felt that Marco needed someone to confide in that day and she had been there; a receptive listener and one he assumed he could trust.

Giles was staring at her, brows drawn and obviously not believing. 'Oh, but surely you have that wrong, my dear! Marco would no more sell the Eagle than—than leave Venice! Hideous as the thing is to me, it's his heritage and he wouldn't dream of selling it; it's the symbol of the Vincella pride, and Marco has that pride in plenty, as you'll have noticed!'

Thankful that they were alone, Jana shook her head and laughed a little uncertainly. 'You're probably right,' she allowed. 'I've got hold of the wrong end of the stick; as you say Marco's got far too much of that Vincella pride to sell the Eagle.' But the damage was done, she realised, when she saw her uncle's expression, and wondered if there was any way she could persuade him not to mention the matter to Marco, as he almost certainly meant to. 'Giles—you won't say anything about this to Marco, will you?'

'About the Eagle? My dear, why on earth should it matter if I mention it when its existence is fairly common knowledge, among historians at any rate?'

Shaking her head, Jana flicked the tip of her tongue anxiously across her lips before she spoke. 'I mean about my telling you that he was thinking of selling it. Please, Giles, I—I don't think he meant me to say anything to anyone else about that.'

Her uncle's face was pale and drawn and she thought he looked incredibly old and ill still, but he was not in any way less sharply aware of her anxiety, and he frowned at her curiously. 'Do you mean that he took you into his confidence about something concerning his family's heirlooms, Jana? Would he do that, my dear? Confide in you alone?'

Jana sat with her hands folded tightly in front of her on the table. It wasn't easy to explain how Marco had come to confide in her, because she wasn't entirely sure herself how it had happened, but she felt so sure that he had trusted her with facts that he did not want generally known that she just had to make her uncle see her position.

'It was one day just before you came out of hospital, when we were having lunch, Giles, he——' she used her hands in a helpless appealing gesture that served no purpose except to show just how much at a loss she felt. 'Oh, I can't explain exactly, but it seemed as if Marco needed someone to talk to about things he had on his mind, and I just happened to be there, that's all it boiled down to. But I wouldn't want him to think that I can't be trusted with a confidence.'

Giles reached over and pressed her hand gently, a faint smile just enough to encourage her. 'I shan't say a word, my dear, you may depend on it! Now—we will pretend that it was never mentioned at all, shall we? It's a hideous creature anyway!'

They were all having breakfast the following morning when Giles congratulated them once more on their achievements during the time he had been in hospital. He smiled from Jana to Marco and back again, making his satisfaction quite obvious. 'You make a very good team, you and Marco, my dear,' he told her, and to Jana his attitude suggested a clue to the original instigator of the idea.

Judging by his evident surprise that they had worked so well together, it had been Marco who proposed the idea and her uncle who went along with it, and she looked across at Giles curiously. 'Didn't you expect us to, Giles?'

Giles was quite frank about it; he caught his friend's eye and pulled a face. 'Quite honestly, my dear, I couldn't see it working out; certainly not as well as it has.'

'I can't think why, Giles.' She carefully avoided looking

at Marco herself and got on with her breakfast while she was talking. 'We're both reasonable, adult people and it was the obvious solution in the circumstances. Marco might not have your professional experience, but he knows Venice inside out and he speaks quite clearly, so I have no difficulty following him. There's no reason why we shouldn't work well together.'

'Oh no, no quite! But—well, you did seem to be a little—wary of Marco at one time, my dear.' The way he laughed suggested that he did not really expect her to follow his meaning, but Jana did, all too easily. Wary was exactly how she had felt about Marco initially.

'I'm more used to him now,' she said by way of explanation, and did not look at Marco when she said it.

'Yes, of course you are, my dear,' her uncle went on, blandly happy with the way things had turned out. 'Thank goodness Marco had enough foresight to realise you'd get used to him and his ways, and insisted on putting the idea to you.'

'Oh, it was Marco's idea, then?'

'Naturally, my dear. I would hardly have asked anyone, even my old friend, to undertake such a task on my behalf.'

'No, of course not.'

Of course he would not have done, she realised, and wondered why that had not occurred to her in the first instance. 'Anyway,' Giles went on determined to give her all the details, 'Marco insisted that you would be prepared to work with him on the project, and you see how well it's worked out, hasn't it? I can scarcely believe you've achieved so much in the time.'

Marco was watching her from the head of the table, his dark eyes as disturbingly steady as always, and she tried to ignore the sensation he aroused in her as she smiled across at her uncle. 'Don't give me too much credit for the amount we've got done, Giles. I simply do as I'm told just as I do

when I work with you. Marco leads the way and I follow—
what's more, he does his own drawings, which are much
better than mine, you'll find!'

'One would expect them to be so in the circumstances,'
Marco's voice interrupted quietly. 'Your own efforts were
excellent, as I remember telling you, but you are not a
trained artist as I am.'

'Yes, of course, my dear, Marco's a trained architect, and
you mustn't belittle your own contribution, you know.'
Once more he sought Marco's support, confident of getting
it. 'I'm sure you'll agree, won't you, Marco, that the task
would be very much harder without Jana's invaluable
help?'

'Very much so, my friend!'

His support was given unhesitatingly, and to her dismay
Jana realised that she was blushing, so that she hastily got
on with her breakfast once more. She was fully aware that
Stefano Abrizzi was taking an interest too, and not appro-
ving either, for she knew what Stefano's feelings were.

He had never made a secret of the fact that he thought
she should have made the most of her uncle's absence to
keep him company instead of working with Marco while he
carried on where her uncle had left off. He would much
rather have taken her sightseeing or gone lazing with her
beside the Lido, and he neither understood nor condoned
her activities on her uncle's behalf. She suspected that he
particularly disliked the fact that she spent so much time in
his cousin's company, though she reminded herself hastily
that he had absolutely no reason to concern himself about
that aspect.

Stefano was young, rich and extremely good-looking, and
he was not accustomed to playing second fiddle to an
academic project or another man; what was more, Jana
suspected he had no intention of doing so for very much
longer. He had attempted to get her alone immediately

before breakfast, just after she left her bedroom, but she had barely time to gather from his whisper in her ear that he was asking her yet again to spend the day with him, when her uncle had joined them.

Frustrated yet again in his efforts to persuade her, he had nevertheless managed to be properly courteous towards her uncle and had escorted them both down to breakfast with his usual smiling charm. But there was a rebellious thrust to his lower lip and his black brows frowned ominously all the time her activities with Marco were under discussion. What he would say, Jana had no idea, but she was not at all surprised when he spoke up at last, and left his opinion in no doubt at all.

'Day after day spent in doing nothing more exciting than looking at the pages of a notebook,' he complained, and Jana saw the way Marco smiled, although he said nothing for the moment. 'Do you not become tired of the history of the Renaissance, Jana?'

'Jana has worked extremely hard on your behalf, Signor Dennis.' Signora Abrizzi's quiet attractive voice interposed hastily, before anyone could take up the point, but Jana guessed that her remark was meant to remind them of how little chance her son had of making headway with his own particular plans for Jana when she was always so involved with her uncle's. 'It is not usual for a young girl to give so much time to the affairs of the past, *signore*; your niece must be very devoted to you.'

Her uncle's slightly shortsighted eyes looked across at Jana fondly, and she knew he understood just how willingly she worked on his behalf. He was not a demonstrative man, but she knew he appreciated what she was doing, even though it might not perhaps be so obvious to someone not familiar with their special rapport.

'I know just how fortunate I am to have someone like Jana to help me, *signora*,' he said, matching her own quiet voice, and he smiled once more at Jana. 'And I am not unappreciative, I assure you.'

'Oh, but of course you are not, *signore*!' The Signora's lovely dark eyes smiled at him in a way that obviously took Giles by surprise, for he hastily swallowed the piece of bread roll he was eating, and reached for his coffee cup. 'You are *simpatica*, I think, eh?'

'I believe that to be just the right word, *signora*.' Giles nodded solemn agreement, a little hesitant about responding to that dazzling smile. 'I know that I wouldn't I couldn't have tackled this project without her. In fact we simply couldn't manage without her, don't you agree, Marco?'

'I could not manage half so well,' Marco agreed. The qualification was typical of him, Jana thought, and barely restrained a smile. He was not the kind of man to readily admit he was too dependent on any woman, it was not his way. 'I would have needed to be both observer and scribe if Jana had not been there to take down my observations, and that would have hindered me considerably.'

'Hanging on your every word, eh?' Giles laughed happily at his own joke, unaware of Marco's swiftly arched brow, although its message served as a reminder to Jana. 'Ah well, she likes nothing better than tramping around ancient buildings and art treasures, do you, my dear? Her enthusiasm and energy are inexhaustible!'

'Not quite inexhaustible, Giles!' She felt rather mean for a moment for denying the boundless energy that he credited her with, but she remembered her rebellious stand a little over a week ago as well as Marco undoubtedly did, and she carefully avoided his eyes while she helped herself to more honey and spread it thickly on a piece of hot roll and butter. 'There's a limit to my endurance—ask Marco!'

Obviously Giles knew nothing of her minor rebellion. She had not told him herself and evidently Marco had said nothing either; in fact the matter would probably never have come to light again if she had not been drawn by her uncle's unstinted praise of her energy and enthusiasm. As it was, Giles was watching her and waiting to be enlightened. Having gone so far, however, she left it to Marco to explain the rest, and he took a long drink from his coffee before he did so.

'It would seem that I am a much harder taskmaster than you are, my friend, and Jana had difficulty in keeping pace with me. She suffered gallantly in your cause for several days, but eventually she rebelled, and put me firmly in my place!'

'Oh, Marco, I *didn't*!' Jana looked down the length of the table at him and frowned indignantly. It wasn't easy to meet his eyes, but just for a second or two she did, and recognised that he was mocking her. 'You're exaggerating it out of all proportion, you know you are! I didn't even try to put you in your place, whatever it may be!' She gave him a swift, meaningful glance from the corner of her eye. 'It would take a bolder woman than I am to put *you* in your place!'

'You think so, *piccina*?' The softness of his voice trickled along her backbone and made her shiver, and she dared not meet his eyes again. 'Do you know me so well, Jana, hm?'

'I didn't—I don't claim to, but I'd never attempt to put you in your place, and you know it!'

'Never attempt to—or never dare to, *piccina*?'

Her brain was spinning chaotically as she tried to follow his reasoning. To think why he was behaving as he was, for he had never before behaved with such embarrassing intimacy, and she could only conclude that in some way it was meant to show Stefano that there was more to their activities than simply taking down notes. He didn't wait for an answer from her, however, but went on with his explanation.

'There was a very pleasant outcome to this—difference, however, Giles, and we are still friends, are we not, Jana?'

'Outcome?' It was Stefano who echoed the provocative word, and his eyes were suspicious, just as if he had the right to be jealous, Jana thought a little dazedly. Things were going rather too swiftly for her at the moment and she wished she was more sure just what Marco was trying to do. 'What was the outcome, Jana?'

'Lunch, *mio caro* Stefano, *naturalmente*.'

Giles caught her eyes and she smiled a little uncertainly. 'First of all I was persuaded to go to the Querini Palace, Giles——'

'Ah, the Palmas—yes, of course!'

'I was absolutely exhausted,' Jana told him, determined to impress him with the true state of affairs, 'and I told Marco I couldn't go on after that, so he took me to lunch.'

'To a little place that I know and the tourists do not,' Marco told her uncle with a half-smile. 'I felt that after having worked so hard, Jana should go somewhere rather special.'

'It was a lovely little spot, Giles, you must try and go there some time. With a balcony overlooking one of the canals and separate little cubicles made by trellis covered in climbing vines and hung over with pot plants.' She was unaware of the warmth that gave her blue eyes the depth of sapphires as she looked along at Marco once more. 'After that I couldn't do anything else but forgive him for walking me off my feet!'

'Ah, I see! Well, there is never any harm in mixing business with a little pleasure, my dear, and you are getting along so very well with the research.'

Giles may have been satisfied with things as they were,

but not so Stefano, Jana thought. He had finished his meal and now sat with his hands clasped together in front of him, his curved thumbs pulling at his lower lip while he regarded her sulkily.

'Work, work, work! *Dio mio*, why must there always be work?'

His dramatic declaration brought an understanding smile from his mother, but she caught Marco's eye and shrugged resignedly when her son went on with his complaint. It was obviously something he had been bursting to say for some time; each time Jana had pleaded being too busy to take time off to go with him on a day's outing, and he was going to have his say now that the opportunity was there.

'*Dio mio*, Jana, you should have time for something other than work! You are a young and lovely woman, and you are in Venice—it is sacrilege to spend so much time writing in a book while Marco makes you walk over the whole city at his heels, like a little puppy-dog running along behind him!'

'Stefano!' Even the Signora was mildly surprised by his vehemence, and she glanced enquiringly at Jana to see if she was taking as much offence as she expected her to. 'Please do not take notice of such nonsense, Jana *mia cara*; please forgive him! *Questo sì che è troppo*, Stefano; *basta!*'

There was a bright gleam in Marco's dark eyes that defied interpretation, but it suggested mockery and it made Jana feel uncomfortable. 'You have a jealous *ammiratore*, Jana, are you not flattered?' His wide mouth curved briefly into a sardonic smile. '*I* am!'

Stefano was angry and also feeling slightly foolish, she thought, but he was determined to stick to his cause and he leaned towards her before he spoke again, although there was little chance of what he said being kept between the two of them only.

'I too know a restaurant, Jana, where it is—rather special?' He used his hands expressively and with the meaning that only a Latin could convey. 'You will come with me for the day, today, hah? And we will enjoy ourselves without any thought of work or of walking around and taking notes! I promise that you shall have lunch without first having to walk all over Venice, eh?'

Stefano in this mood was irresistible and well aware of it, but she had arranged with Marco to visit the Church of the Frari to see a particularly fine altarpiece by Titian, and she did not like to suggest changing his plans simply so that she could go off and enjoy herself with Stefano. It was a delicate situation, but much as she admitted to being tempted, she could not quite see how she was going to handle it at the moment.

'I'd like to, of course, Stefano——'

'Then why do you not go, Jana *mia cara*?'

Once more Signora Abrizzi spoke up on her son's behalf, but it was much more difficult to guess how Marco was taking it and Jana looked at him for a moment from the shadow of her lashes before she said anything. From his expression it might be supposed that he did not care either way whether she accepted Stefano's invitation, but she could not see his eyes, and she always liked to judge what Marco was thinking by what she saw in those dark expressive eyes of his.

'Jana my dear,' Giles said, obviously in two minds himself, 'of course I don't begrudge you a day off, you know that, but Marco has been good enough to take over from me and has worked so hard on my project, that I think you should consider him too. He's made some arrangements for today and I feel it isn't right to simply drop the whole thing without warning.'

'Oh no, of course not, Giles!' Jana looked again at the dark and severely handsome face at the top of the table and felt rather like a schoolgirl asking to miss class. 'Marco, I know you've made some arrangements for today, but would it inconvenience you *very* much if we postponed it and I went out with Stefano for the day?'

He looked up, the dark eyes catching her uncertain gaze before she could look away, and there was a curiously disturbing gleam in their depths that she found oddly affecting. 'I enjoy acting for Giles and delight in having such a charming companion, so it would not be fair of me to deny my cousin the same pleasure, would it? You do not need my permission to go with Stefano, *piccina*, if that is what you would rather do.'

The compliment was, in this instance, both unexpected and rather touching in a way she could not explain, and she found herself seriously wondering if she *did* prefer to go with Stefano; something she would not even have thought twice about only a couple of weeks ago. But Stefano had inevitably noted the slight flush in her cheeks and briefly caught his mother's eye as he raised a brow.

He resented the idea of not being accepted without hesitation, it was clear, just as he resented having been pulled up for his rash observation about her situation with Marco, and it showed in his eyes. '*Là*,' he said with heavy sarcasm, 'you have Marco's permission, Jana, now you may come with me, eh?'

'I'd like to, Stefano, thank you.'

She refused to be ruffled by his sarcasm and she guessed he was already regretting it, despite the hint of sulkiness about his mouth. She as well as Stefano looked up quickly when Marco added a proviso that was completely unexpected, a glint of black warning in his eyes.

'You have Jana's company for today, Stefano; tomorrow I will require her once more, for we have much to do and I cannot work without her help.'

If it had been a deliberate attempt to rouse Stefano's anger, it could not have been more successful, for his good-looking features flushed and his eyes were bright as gems as he glared at Marco without speaking for a moment. 'Of course, Marco, I understand that Jana looks upon you as a substitute for her uncle—I will not forget!'

Marco said nothing; he simply looked down the length of the table and caught Jana's eye before she could look away, and he smiled.

Because Jana had expressed a preference for it, they had taken a gondola for the first part of their trip, the most expensive form of travel in Venice, but still the most romantic and the most typically Venetian to Jana's mind, and to Stefano too, apparently, for he fell in with the idea without hesitation.

Stefano knew nothing of the history of the city and made no apology for it; he was a man of today and saw no need to dwell on past glories, nor to mourn the possible loss of so much beauty if the worst should happen and Venice was no more, not the way Marco did. In this Jana found it hard to be in harmony with him, although she enjoyed his company in every other way.

He was Venetian born, but most of his life had been spent in the various capitals of Europe while his parents moved from one country to another. He had had a cosmopolitan upbringing and yet he was still essentially Italian, if not Venetian, in character; his international education had merely honed a sharper edge on his Italian charm. A charm that Jana suspected he knew how to use to his best advantage.

He took every opportunity to squeeze her hand, or to put an arm about her shoulders as they walked; wandering through the narrow *calli* close together, weaving from one to the other and avoiding the most tourist-crowded ones, and Jana responded in the way she was bound to, the way Stefano expected her to.

She revelled in the warm, sensuous charm of him because he was so different from anyone she had ever known before, and he charmed her with practised ease, in a way she knew she was not expected to take seriously. He sought out little *campielli* that were quiet and shaded and much more attractive than the bigger squares with their crowds of summer tourists.

In one of the small *campielli* they found a café and sat outside at a tiny table that brought them close together; and there they drank excellent coffee while Stefano held her hand and gazed at her with an earnestness that made her heart flutter. She had spent so much time with the past lately that at the moment she felt she had almost forgotten the freedom of flirting with a good-looking man of her own age.

'You are very beautiful, Jana—*molta bella, cara mia*!' He pressed his lips to the backs of her hands and gazed at her with dark gleaming eyes, his fingers strong and firm about hers. 'I have hated it these past weeks when Marco has taken you away from me every day to walk you around and around while you write in your little book! *Dio mio*!— such a waste!'

His eyes were warmly persuasive and it was hard for her to believe that she had known him such a short time. Not that knowing him was necessary to the kind of intimacy that Stefano's eyes suggested, and she felt a small shiver of sensation slip along her spine almost like a warning as she looked across into that smoothly handsome face.

'You do not always like to be writing in your little book, do you, Jana?'

His smooth brown fingers played with hers while he

spoke and their caressing touch made it difficult for her to answer as coolly as she hoped to. 'I don't mind at all, in fact I quite enjoy it.'

She had spoken the truth almost without realising it, for she did enjoy doing what she did, although Stefano obviously did not believe it, for he made a sound with his mouth that dismissed the very idea as unlikely. '*Non posso crederlo!*' he insisted, his fingers squeezing hard. 'You cannot mean that you enjoy being taken by Marco like a schoolgirl, around all the old buildings. No, *bella mia*, I do not believe it!'

It was an impulse that made her speak as she did, prompted by something she thought she saw in his eyes for a second when he spoke of his cousin. 'Don't you like your cousin?'

'Marco?' He looked vaguely surprised at being expected to answer a question like that, and he gave a second or two to his answer, as if he had never before considered it. '*Sì, mi piace*—but I do not like him when he takes you out every day and I am left to——'

'Sulk?' Jana suggested softly, unable to resist it, and Stefano frowned indignantly when she smiled.

He held her hands with crushing tightness and once more raised them to his lips, pressing a series of light kisses on her open palms, then folding her fingers over and holding them tightly between his own while he looked into her eyes. 'You are cruel, *bella mia*, hah? You laugh at me when I am trying to tell you how much I have wanted to take you from Marco these past weeks. Do you feel nothing for me?'

He was well aware that wasn't so, Jana knew, and her senses were too responsive to his determined charm. He knew just how fascinating he was, and just how most women would respond to his insistence, but he must also know that his cousin had a very virile and mature fascination too, and Jana had been in Marco's company for hours at a time. It was the extent of Marco's fascination that he sought to discover and to overcome.

'I like you, Stefano, I like you quite a lot, in fact.' She felt curiously and pedantically English suddenly as she tried to put what she felt into words, and it was not made easier by the dark eyes that watched her so closely. 'But I don't know——'

'*No, no, no, cara mia!*' He placed a finger firmly over her lips to silence her at the same time bringing his face closer to hers and gazing directly into her eyes. 'That you like me I know,' he assured her with no trace of embarrassment or false humility. 'That is a beginning, but soon I will make you feel something much more exciting than like, *bella mia!*' He raised her hands to his lips once more and kissed them, keeping hold of them while he pulled her to her feet and guided her round the little table until they stood face to face on the shadowed paving. 'Soon, *carissima*, hah?'

It was inevitable, Jana thought, and found herself quite in favour of the idea as they walked through the *campiello* hand in hand. 'I don't know how easy it will be getting another day off just yet, Stefano, there's still an awful lot of work to do before Giles can actually begin writing the book.' Then catching his eye, she smiled. 'But I expect I can beg some time occasionally.'

Stefano's brown fingers squeezed cruelly hard and brought a murmur of protest from her. 'Of whom do you beg for time, *cara mia*?' he asked in a voice suddenly edged with sharpness. 'Your uncle or Marco, hmm?'

It was an oddly discomfiting question to answer and Jana took a moment to remind herself that she would need to consult both her mentors. 'Possibly both,' she told him after a moment or two. 'Giles is the one most concerned, of course, but Marco's been doing most of the work lately and

I can hardly leave him to manage on his own in the circumstances.'

'And he will not let you go!' She looked at him to deny it, but Stefano was shaking his head firmly, and she knew in her heart he was right, though for other reasons than the ones Stefano obviously credited him with. 'I know Marco and he does not easily let go—what he has he holds!'

Jana was reminded of the Vincella Eagle, and she shook her head to dismiss that disturbing thought. 'He's not unreasonable, Stefano, but he does have the right to my support when he's doing so much for Giles.' She laughed, remembering how Marco had rushed her around at first. 'He works much more quickly than Giles does, so it may not be as long as we anticipate before we finish!'

That in turn gave rise to other possibilities and Stefano drew her into the shadows, holding both her hands while she faced him, his dark eyes sweeping over her face before he spoke. 'When you finish this—notebook, Jana, will your uncle then wish to return to England to write his book?'

Unsure of the answer, she shook her head. 'I don't know, possibly he will.'

'Dannazione!' Stefano swore softly to himself, then shook his head when he realised she was looking at him curiously. 'You must not be gone before the ballo di costume, Jana. I wish you to be here for that!'

Jana did a hasty translation and realised that he referred to the costume ball that Marco had told her about. He too had expressed a hope that she would be there, in fact he had been most insistent that she should be there or Stefano would be very disappointed. She nodded understanding. 'Oh yes, the party that Marco told me about—I remember.'

Stefano's dark eyes narrowed suspiciously. 'He has already invited you?'

'He said I should be there,' she explained, not looking at him and choosing her words very carefully because she remembered how much she had disliked Marco's intimation that it would be Stefano who was going to be disappointed if she did not go, and not himself. 'He said you'd be very disappointed if I didn't go.'

'And so I should be, *carissima*!' He raised her hands to his lips and kissed her fingers. 'But you will be there, will you not, Jana? And you and I will complement each other with our costumes, eh? We will go as a couple, someone very—*romantica*, hah?'

He squeezed her hand hard and she glanced up swiftly when they were suddenly plunged into almost darkness. A narrow passageway connected the *campiello* with one of the bigger squares and her eyes glowed in the dimness as she looked along to where the sun awaited them at the other end. 'I don't think I'll tell you what I'm going as,' she told him, and laughed softly when he frowned. 'I shan't tell anyone!'

'You do not wish to be my partner?'

Their footsteps echoed slightly against the curved roof of the archway, and she watched the light grow on the cold stone walls as they neared the sunlit square. 'I'd like to be just whoever I feel like being,' she told him, 'and I shall keep it a secret until the very last minute!'

'You will not even tell me?'

She shook her head. 'I won't even tell—Giles.'

She had so very nearly said Marco that the realisation startled her, and she felt a hard rapid beat in her heart as she walked out into the sunshine once more. As if Marco would care anyway!

CHAPTER FIVE

It was rather early to be taking a break, Jana supposed, but to her at least the respite was very welcome even though they had not achieved very much so far that morning. Venice was in the throes of high summer and shimmered with the heat, also most of the places they wanted to visit were crowded with visitors and consequently their task was made a hundred times more difficult.

If only Giles had given more thought to the timing of his visit and come either early in the year, or later on towards the end it would have been much less arduous. But Giles was a creature of impulse, and the fact that he did not have to trouble himself with finding accommodation in one of the crowded hotels had made him oblivious to the fact that the height of the tourist season was not the best time to be doing the rounds of galleries, churches and museums, until it was too late.

Sitting in the cool and drinking coffee was much more desirable than trying to make notes while being jostled by passing sightseers and distracted by the buzz of multi-lingual chatter. It had been in Jana's mind for some time now whether or not to mention the Vincella Eagle again. She had never denied her curiosity, but so far it had received little satisfaction, and she had not yet been given a glimpse of the historic symbol of the Vincella, although it was probably her own fault that she hadn't, she supposed.

Once or twice, when she had been with Stefano on one of their rare evening dates, she had been tempted to ask him about the Eagle, but somehow something had always stopped her from saying anything at the last minute. Sitting here with Marco was really an ideal time to bring the subject up if she had a mind to, and she had been musing on the wisdom of doing so ever since they sat down.

At first she told herself, as she had told Giles, that if Marco had wanted her to see it he would have shown it to her when he first mentioned its existence, but he had said nothing about it since then and, perhaps because of his silence on the subject, she had said nothing more herself. However, neither her own nor Marco's reticence had done anything to diminish her curiosity and today she thought she might mention in passing that she would very much like to see it, if it was possible. She would take a roundabout route, of course, rather than ask him outright, but she thought she might ask him today.

Drinking coffee was a favourite Venetian pastime that Jana heartily approved of, and one that Marco was much more inclined to indulge in since he had relaxed their earlier strenuous routine. There were so many delightful little cafés that provided not only an excellent coffee, but also a chance to sit and gaze at some of Venice's many beautiful buildings while refreshing oneself.

They had seldom visited the same one twice so far, and their number seemed endless; sometimes they were so small that there were no more than three or four tables set out in some quiet little *campo*, yet the service and the excellence of the coffee they served was of the same high standard. Like a true Venetian, Marco seemed to know them all.

The present one was very like the one Stefano had taken her to, but this time her companion was keeping his distance rather than holding her hands as Stefano had. Yet for all that there was a warmth in Marco's dark eyes that had much the same effect as Stefano's physical touch, and she found him just as disturbing—or more so.

A brown silk shirt complemented his olive-dark complexion and was matched perfectly with well-cut fawn slacks and soft brown leather shoes that looked as if they were hand-made. His black hair just brushed the collar of his shirt and swept back from the broad impressive brow because he had only a moment since run his fingers through it.

To Jana the shadowed brown throat still looked incredibly vulnerable where it emerged from an open neck, despite the general impression of physical strength—or perhaps because of it. It seemed to be the one pregnable thing about his whole physical make-up, and Jana found her gaze drawn to it again and again, without knowing why it held such a fascination for her.

Running a light finger-tip around the rim of her coffee cup, she approached the subject of the Vincella Eagle cautiously. 'I was thinking about the Vincella Eagle,' she ventured. 'The one you told me about, if you remember.'

'There is only the one, Jana, and of course I remember telling you about it.'

Not exactly encouraging, Jana thought, but she went on nevertheless. 'It must be a terrific responsibility, having it there in the *palazzo*, I mean. If you say it's worth about two million lire, I would have thought a bank vault or somewhere like that was a safer place.'

Her reason for mentioning it obviously made him curious, and he was looking at her questioningly. 'But there are many such treasures housed in *palazzi* all over Venice, Jana, and most of them are on display. The Eagle is at least locked away, there is little fear of it being stolen by any thieves.'

'Locked away where no one can see it,' she observed, and realised at once that he followed her meaning without effort.

Regarding her for a moment in speculative silence while he drank more of his coffee, he flicked an enquiring brow at her. 'You wish to see it?' he asked.

She had not expected him to be quite so forthright, and she was at a loss for a moment, unsure what to say. If he had asked her the same question immediately after telling her of the Eagle's existence she would not have hesitated, as it was she was bound to wonder if he saw her barely concealed hint as presumptuous, and she took her time answering.

'I wasn't—fishing for an invitation from you to show it to me,' she told him, though she doubted if he believed the untruth, he was far too shrewd for that. 'It's just that it's a fascinating subject and having something as valuable as that in your home must be quite a headache. I'd love to have seen it, of course——'

'Then of course you shall see it, *piccina*!' He caught her eye and smiled, still in two minds about something, she guessed, although whether he questioned her temerity in bringing the matter up, or her reluctance to admit it, she could not guess at the moment. 'Did you really think I would *not* be willing to show it to you, Jana?'

'It was possible. After all, you told me about the Eagle a good two weeks ago now, and you haven't once mentioned it since.'

'And you have been burning with feminine curiosity for two whole weeks, eh, *piccina*?'

It was hard to meet his eyes in the circumstances, and Jana sought refuge in defensiveness. 'Curiosity isn't a feminine prerogative,' she told him. 'But since you raise the question—yes, I am curious about the Eagle, I have been ever since you told me about it. Naturally I assume you have it under lock and key and only bring it out on special occasions—I can understand that.'

'And your—curiosity shall make it a special occasion,' Marco assured her. 'For you I will unlock it and you shall have your wish to see it.'

'Thank you, that's very good of you.'

She sounded very formal and rather stiff, she realised, and sensed rather than saw the swiftly arched black brow that commented on it. 'You will possibly agree with Giles that it is ugly,' he told her, 'but it is impressive even though it is not beautiful, and it has an—a feeling about it, hah?'

It was so seldom that his English failed him that Jana could not resist supplying the word he sought. 'An aura?' she suggested, and he nodded.

'*Sì ciò è retto*, it has an aura.'

'An aura of power?' Jana had no real idea why she said that, but it was something that came immediately to mind when she thought of the massive stone replica with a struggling man in its power. 'It just struck me that it symbolises power,' she explained hastily, and once more Marco nodded agreement.

'You are possibly correct, *piccina*, for the Vincella have been very powerful in the past.'

'Not in the present too?'

She had seen him as a power in his own right, though of course not in the old way. But he was wealthy and influential, and surely no past Vincella had possessed more of that almost ruthless pride than the present holder of the title did. The idea seemed to need some consideration as far as Marco was concerned, however, for he took a moment to think about it, then shook his head firmly.

'Not any more,' he declared.

Leaning his elbows on the table, he gazed at the little *campo* tucked away off the more busy tourist routes. It was surrounded by tall buildings that cast their long shadows inwards from two sides, drawn on the heat-shimmering surface of the square like the hours on a clock face. While across on the other side, where they sat protected by a striped awning, the air was hot and lazy, disturbed only by the abstract buzz of activity in nearby, busier squares, and the barely definable sound of water that was never very far away in Venice.

From a nearby *campanile* a chime rang out and was echoed by others, clear and sharp on the heat-muffled air. Emerging from the shadows across the square, a couple strolled across with their arms twined about one another and their eyes aware only of each other; bodies close and touching, conscious of their closeness and nothing else. And as he swept his gaze over and past them, Mario caught Jana's eye and smiled.

'*Romantico, sì?*' he asked, brows arched quizzically.

'Honeymooners?' Jana suggested, an unaccountable warmth in her cheeks, and Marco's brief smile mocked her.

'Or simply lovers?' he countered softly.

'Maybe.' She followed the young couple's progress across the *campo* with a curious and inexplicable sense of envy. 'They look English.'

Marco's dark eyes seemed to mock both her reluctance to recognise them as simply lovers and her reasoning, and he shook his head slowly. 'Are the English, then, incapable of being lovers?' he asked, and she shook her head hastily to deny it while remaining silent. He continued to study her with the same slow, speculative gaze for several seconds more, then startled her with the touch of a long forefinger tracing lightly along her bare arm. 'Do you not have an English lover who is missing you, Jana, hmm?'

Taken by surprise she shook her head again, conscious of a sudden more urgent beat to her heart. 'I had a boy-friend, but there's no one serious.'

'Ah!' He continued to study her with that slow speculative gaze as if he sought to know her better. 'Is he not important enough for you to wish to return to him, *piccola*, eh? He must surely be missing you very much after all this time.'

The last thing in the world that Jana wanted to do was to

sit in a quiet sunlit square and discuss her former boy-friend with him, and she shrugged uneasily as she sought an answer. 'Possibly,' she allowed. 'Although I haven't heard from him since I came to Venice, so I don't think he can be suffering too much, somehow!'

The dark eyes between their thick lashes gleamed with a hint of malice for a moment, and a sardonic smile gave a touch of cruelty to his mouth. 'Perhaps,' he suggested, soft-voiced, 'the English *are* incapable of being lovers, eh, Jana?'

'Not at all!' She made the denial swiftly and instinc-tively without really thinking about it; anxious only to deny the shortcomings of her fellow-countrymen. Shaking her head slowly, she cast him a vaguely reproachful look from beneath half-lowered lids, but hastily looked away again. 'It's simply that I don't like—I'm not in the habit of dis-cussing things like that.'

'Ah! You find it—embarrassing? I am sorry!'

'Not necessarily embarrassing, Marco, it's just that——' She shrugged once more, finding that most Latin of gest-ures increasingly useful. 'I suppose I'm just too English to find it easy discussing a boy-friend with a stranger.'

'A stranger.' He mused on the word and seemed to dis-like it, for he was frowning. 'I suppose that is what I am, eh, Jana?'

'Oh, but I didn't mean——' She stopped herself hastily, biting her lip in her anxiety not to be misunderstood, then she laughed, a small and shiveringly uneasy sound, as she looked across at him. 'I don't really think of you as a stranger, Marco, nor do I feel strange in Venice now,' she confessed in a slightly breathless voice. 'In fact I find it hard sometimes to imagine living anywhere else, and I haven't been here quite a month yet!' Gazing across the *campo* with its shimmering pattern of shadows, she shook her head. 'I've got used to a completely different way of life much more quickly than I'd have believed I could.'

'You throw in your whole heart, do you not, *piccina*?' The dark eyes sought and held hers, while that hypnotic finger still traced its way with thrilling lightness over her soft skin. 'And you do not wish to leave, do you, Jana?'

Frowning slightly, she wondered if the question had any significance, and she hesitated. 'We're *not* leaving; not yet, are we?' she asked. There was a suggestion of huskiness in her voice and she could not imagine how anxiously she looked at him. 'I mean, Giles hasn't suggested that we go home until he's well enough to get around again himself?'

'No, *piccina*, he has not.' She tried in vain not to look directly at him, but somehow she seemed to have no choice, and her hands were trembling as she held her coffee cup tightly in both hands. 'And you will know that I have not made such a suggestion, *sì*?'

'No. No, of course you haven't, but I just wondered——'

'If your slightly unreal new world was about to suffer a mortal blow, eh, Jana?'

Jana wished she did not feel so horribly vulnerable, and it put her on the defensive without her realising it. 'I don't know what you and Giles might have concocted between you,' she told him. 'It was you, after all, who arranged for us to work together while Giles was in hospital, no one said anything to me until it was a—*fait accompli*. How would I know whether or not you've come to some other arrangement without telling me.'

'We have not, that I promise you, Jana—and it works well, you and I, *sì*?'

'It works very well, I have to agree, even though Giles didn't expect it to.'

Marco watched her closely, his eyes slightly mocking, like his smile. 'Even though you did not expect it to either, eh, Jana?'

How could she deny it? She had been wary, just as Giles

said, and Marco knew it as well as anyone did. 'No. No, I admit I didn't expect it to either, but I'll be the first to admit it has.'

'You enjoy working with me, do you not?'

He traced an imaginary line from her elbow to her wrist on the soft, sensitive skin of her inner arm, and she barely controlled a shiver from her too responsive senses. 'Yes, of course I do, Marco, we get along very well together.'

'*Molto bene*,' Marco agreed soft-voiced. 'So why do you imagine that Giles would bring our partnership to an end when we still have so much to do, eh?'

'No—no, he wouldn't, of course.'

Her cup was empty and Jana had a sudden almost panicky urge to leave the small quiet square while she still had control over her emotions; moving her arm from that light, evocative touch was the first deliberate move. Holding her handbag tightly in both hands she pushed back her chair and shook back the golden hair from her flushed face.

'Which reminds me,' she said breathlessly and too quickly, 'we've done very little this morning and we've been sitting here for ages! We'll never get through that schedule you've prepared for us if we sit here wasting time like this instead of getting on!'

She was almost sure he frowned, but she did not look at him to know how right she was, and after a second or two he stood up, offering her his hand with his usual unfailing courtesy. But in her anxiety to control her own emotions she had been too abrupt, too insensitive to his, and there was a cool hard edge on his voice that Jana regretted more than she cared to admit at the moment.

'*Naturalmente*, you do not wish to waste any more time on such trivial matters! I apologise for delaying us, Jana; let us go, hah?'

They crossed the square side by side but not close together; not touching, even where their hands swung be-

tween them in unison, and recalling the young couple who
had passed them earlier Jana experienced that brief, inexplicable feeling of envy once more.

The Gothic beauty of Santa Maria Gloriosa dei Frari was
behind them, Titian's glorious representation of the As-
sumption duly noted as one of the things Giles insisted
must be included, and they had visited a couple of other
churches in the same area before Jana eventually called a
halt. She was hot and tired, and she suspected Marco was
quite deliberately making things harder for her, so that she
looked reproachfully at him when he obediently stopped in
the shadow of the Torre dell'Orologio, a fifteenth-century
clock tower that might well have qualified for their notes on
Renaissance.

They were in the dazzling, tourist-packed Piazza San
Marco, and she had to stand fairly close to him while she
declared her intention of going no further, because there
were so many people about. Being so close made it necessary for her to tip back her head to look at his face, and she
caught a brief but unmistakable glint of amusement in his
eyes that made her frown.

'You're paying me back, aren't you, Marco?' she ac-
cused, keeping her voice as low as the volume of human
voices around them allowed, and Marco looked down at her
steadily for a second before he replied.

'Paying you back?' He repeated the sentence as if he had
no idea of its meaning, although she felt pretty sure that his
English was well up to coping with anything as common-
place as that. 'What do you mean, Jana?'

Something made her hesitate to give him the obvious and
literal meaning, and instead she shook her head and looked
anywhere but at him for the moment. 'Oh, it doesn't
matter! But I *am* tired and hungry, Marco, and it's time
we finished for this morning.'

'Ah, you now consider that we have done enough work for one morning, is that it?'

She looked around her at the crowded square and tried to stay out of the sun. 'We've done far more than we usually do in a morning,' she insisted, 'you know we have, Marco, and it's so hot.'

Tiredness combined with uncertainty made her sound faintly petulant and she thought she saw him smile briefly as he registered the fact. 'Venice is usually hot in mid-June, Jana, there is nothing I can do about that, but if you find the pace too gruelling for you we must take more time with our afternoon schedule. I was simply trying to get through our programme as quickly as possible since it seemed to be your wish to do so.'

Unconvinced, Jana said nothing for a moment. She had never seen him vengeful before, but when she thought about it it was well in character for the man she had first thought him. He had not liked her cutting short that dangerously intimate conversation as they sat in the café in the square, when she had urged him to get on with their schedule, and he had let her know it. He had complied with her suggestion that they get on instead of lingering over coffee and pleasant conversation, but he had done so with such relentless energy that she was exhausted.

Looking up at him once more, she shook her head. 'I know why you decided to revert to your original killing pace,' she told him, 'and I suppose in a way it was my fault——'

'It was your own suggestion, *piccina*!'

'But I must take a break now, Marco, really; you've walked me off my feet this morning!'

Dark eyes scanned her flushed cheeks for a moment slowly, noting the slightly rebellious pout to her mouth and the long lashes that hid her eyes from him once more, and he smiled. '*Benissimo!*' His hand slid beneath her arm and the fingers were as light as a caress on her skin, then he turned her in the direction of the nearest *vaporetto* station. 'We shall go home, eh?'

'Yes, of course. We usually do, don't we?'

Inexplicably she felt disappointed, although she had not really expected him to take her to lunch again as he had the first time she complained. But it was almost as if he sensed her mood, for he stopped and turned to look down into her face suddenly, a hint of smile on his mouth.

'Or will you come with me to Il Giardino?'

She would go anywhere he took her, Jana knew that, but she had an idea that the restaurant he named was the same one he had taken her to the last time, and she nodded without hesitation. 'Isn't that where we went before? The one with the separate tables with trellis between and flowers?'

'*Sì*, you enjoyed it there, did you not?'

'Very much, it was lovely! I'd love to go again, Marco, please!'

'Then I shall take you again, *piccola*, if it makes you so happy.'

Briefly the suggestion of almost paternal indulgence in his tone made her frown, but the thought of lunching in those delightful surroundings once more was worth swallowing a little indignity for, and she hastened to keep pace with him as he headed towards the nearest *vaporetto* station.

Marco seldom used the *vaporetto*, although Jana always rather enjoyed it. Its discomforts were much the same as those of the rush-hour at home, but the setting as well as the atmosphere was much different, and although the crowd jostled and pushed for places it was for the most part good-natured and had none of the rather grim reserve of a London rush-hour crowd.

Inevitably there were no seats, so that they were obliged to stand, close together and sandwiched between a large woman with a shopping basket that pressed into Jana's back and an equally large man who, although he was a good foot shorter than Marco, made up for his lack of inches in bulk.

The *vaporetto* was soon under way and as they left the station Jana felt a hand slide around her waist and draw her close until she was firmly held against the lean hard warmth of Marco's body, his long fingers spread out over her back and the palm pressing warmly against her through the thin summer dress she wore.

Her face came somewhere in the region of the vee where his shirt opened, and she was made breathtakingly aware of the smooth tanned chest it exposed, of the heat of his body mingling with masculine scents, spicy and tantalising to her senses. Something made her glance up after a moment and she caught the bright disturbing gleam in his eyes looking directly at her, so that she hastily looked away again. The shirt he wore was silk, soft and smooth against her cheek when she lowered her head, and she caught her breath when the warmth of his tanned skin touched her through the thin material.

'Almost there.'

His voice spoke softly against her ear and she supposed he was apologising in a way. Then the stout woman's basket was removed from her back at the second stop and the next one to that saw the departure of the stout man, so that they had more breathing space, but the hand at Jana's back still kept its hold on her, and she found herself not at all averse to the sensation it aroused.

Two more stops and then Marco was helping her up the steps to the wide *fondamenta*, keeping hold of her hand while they walked the paved path beside the canal until they turned into a *campo* that she thought was vaguely familiar. Another turn and another, through one cool, narrow *calle* after another, and across small arched bridges that were spangled underneath with reflected sunlight off the water, until they turned into one narrow *rughetta* that she remembered very well from their last visit.

It was lined on both sides by tall buildings that gave her the feeling of walking along the bottom of a deep canyon, and so narrow that the shadows fell not only across the road but also splashed up on to the mellow stone walls of the houses opposite like spilled black ink. There was a curious suggestion of blankness about them too, for here, as in the rest of Venice, all the buildings presented their best face to the water.

It was as they turned from the *rughetta* and into an arched passageway out of the sunlight for a moment that Marco turned to her and smiled. 'Do you still think that you could find your way here without me, Jana?' he asked with that now familiar hint of mockery.

Convinced that she could not, Jana shook her head. 'I'm quite certain I couldn't!' She did not add that she could not imagine herself ever coming there alone or with anyone else, but looked up at him and smiled when she found herself suddenly dazzled by the return of sunlight as they emerged from the passageway. 'But I remember these old steps!'

Leading up from the *fondamenta* on which the restaurant was built, the winding steps were narrow enough to make her cling tightly to Marco's guiding hand, and a moment later they walked on to the small terrace with its dividing trellises wound round with vines and hung with pots of flowers. It was hardly likely, she thought, that they were expected, and yet from Lucio's manner it would seem that they were, and the proprietor led them to the same table they had been given the last time they were there.

'I shall choose for you, *sì*?' This time Marco made no attempt to give her the menu, but arched a brow at her, and she nodded.

'Yes, please—and I'm hungry!'

'I remember!' He consulted the menu, then turned once more to Lucio. The man's lean solemn face was the most serious one Jana had yet seen in Venice, but he was courteous and attentive and Jana was in no mood to see fault in anyone at the moment. 'For the *signorina, prosciutto crudo con melone*, and for myself *seppie, per piacere, scampi giganti per due persone* and—some fruit, I think, eh, Jana?' He almost took her nod of agreement for granted. 'And we will have the *vino di casa*, Lucio, *per favore*.'

Jana would never have dreamed of ordering raw ham for herself, but sliced tissue-thin and served with slices of melon it was delicious, and looked much more appetising than Marco's squid cooked in its own ink. The scampi were huge and served in their own shells, their flavour enhanced by a bright, light wine, the speciality of the house. They were sharing a dish of fresh peaches and figs when Marco suddenly lifted his head sharply as if something had caught his attention.

She frowned across at him curiously for a second then, as she was about to question his obvious interest in what was going on out of sight on the terrace, she thought she recognised one of the voices. Slightly raised, apparently in annoyance and speaking in Italian, she nevertheless recognised it after a second or two as Stefano's, and the mention a few seconds later of 'il Conte di Vincella' confirmed her recognition.

Stefano, too, obviously knew of this very special restaurant, and as far as she could gather he was asking for Marco. But if she could make little of the spate of Italian, obviously Marco could, and he murmured an apology to her, then got to his feet and stepped around the edge of the trellis screen into view. Tall and autocratic, he spoke with that air of command that seemed to come naturally to him.

'*Che cos'è*, Lucio?'

'Ah, *signore*!'

Lucio, the proprietor, obviously welcomed his appearance and a further spate of rapid Italian followed, kept at a discreet level for the benefit of the other clients. He was silenced after a few moments by Marco's raised hand, and Marco addressed himself to Stefano in short, sharp sentences that suggested impatience as much as anger, though he too kept his voice low.

'Jana?'

She heard Stefano echo her name and there followed a rather awkward silence that lasted for a second or two, then a woman's voice intervened, sharp and questioning, and Stefano laughed. He was not so much amused as embarrassed, Jana gathered, and she wondered what Marco had said to him. Another few words were exchanged, and then footsteps tapped across the stone terrace towards the steps, the woman's voice protesting volubly until distance silenced it. Marco came back to their table, but he had barely time to sit down before Lucio appeared, his long solemn face looking vaguely apologetic.

'*Chiedo perdono, signore, non so*——'

'You could not be expected to know that Signor Abrizzi was also coming, Lucio. Do not concern yourself, *per piacere*, there is no harm done!'

'*Grazie, signore.*'

He left them, and as soon as he was out of sight behind the vine-covered trellis, Jana looked across curiously at Marco. Obviously the unexpected arrival of his cousin had affected his mood, and she was in two minds whether or not to ask him the reason, but when he poured them both more wine, then looked across and caught her eye, she smiled instinctively.

'Trouble?' she asked, and Marco shrugged his shoulders as expressively as only a Latin could.

'Stefano had taken the liberty of asking for a table to be reserved in my name. It is difficult if you are not well known here to simply be given a table on demand, and finding me already here he was a little—put out.'

'Oh, I see.' She recalled a fleeting impression of Lucio's manner when they arrived. 'I had a feeling when we appeared that Lucio had been expecting us,' she said. 'That would explain it.'

His dark eyes held hers for a moment, slightly narrowed and fathomless as pools of dark water when she tried to read something into them. 'He was not alone, Jana.'

He said it as if he expected some emotional reaction from her, and she did not quite understand him. He should have known his cousin well enough to know he was unlikely to go anywhere in public without a woman on his arm, and she shook her head and smiled as she spun the stem of her wine glass between her fingers, and watched the soft golden liquid catching the sunlight.

'I'm hardly surprised,' she said. 'Stefano isn't the solitary type and he knows I'm working with you this morning; it's one of his most frequent complaints, that I spend most of my time working.'

'He wished you to come here with him today?'

'Probably, if he'd ordered a table.' In fact Stefano had asked her immediately after breakfast to take time off from work and have lunch with him, but he had made no mention of this specific restaurant and she very much doubted if she would have answered any differently if he had. 'He did ask me to have lunch with him, as a matter of fact, but I told him I was going to be busy and——' She shrugged and laughed a little uncertainly. 'Well, he wasn't very pleased; but you must know better than I do that Stefano doesn't like being told he can't have what he wants, when he wants it.'

'You find him spoiled?'

Jana wasn't sure if she should put it quite as strongly as that, for Marco was very fond of his cousin even though he did not see eye to eye with him on a number of matters. He was his family and the Italian takes his family very seriously, she knew.

'It's understandable that he's used to getting his own way,' she said, choosing not to agree with his uncompromising frankness. 'He's an only child of wealthy parents and it's natural that he's had everything he wants all his life.' She smiled when she recalled Stefano's irresistible charm. 'But he'd be just as charming whatever his circumstances, I'm sure; Stefano's a born charmer!'

'And, as you have said, he is accustomed to having what he wants.' Marco's expression was thoughtful and there were deep lines at the corners of his mouth that gave the sternly handsome face yet more character. Not a charmer in the same sense of the word as Stefano was, but a virile and mature man with a magnetism of his own that was just as effective as his cousin's—perhaps even more so. He caught her gaze once more and looked directly into her eyes for a moment before he spoke again. 'At the moment it is you that he wants, Jana, you know that, do you not?'

It was a startlingly frank question and not an easy one to answer, and Jana knew she was blushing like a schoolgirl. She also knew he was right about Stefano, but just as right to make the proviso 'at the moment', for she did not fool herself that Stefano's apparently ardent wooing of her was done with any permanent liaison in mind. That just wasn't Stefano's way, not with girls like Jana. One day no doubt he would marry, but someone suitable to his life-style. Pretty *and* rich, for Stefano's taste would always run to the extravagant.

'I wonder if he'd be half so keen,' she ventured after a second or two, 'if I wasn't always too busy to go out with him just whenever he feels like it—if I was more available.'

'I believe he would.' He spoke quietly and with that

certain timbre in his voice that sent curious little trickling sensations all through her body when she heard it. Leaning as he was, with his elbows on the table in front of him, his face was quite close and she could not miss the dark intensity in his eyes when he looked at her. 'You do yourself an injustice, Jana, as well as Stefano. He is a lover of beautiful things, like most Venetians, and he would find you irresistible for that reason alone.'

Remembering the female voice she had heard during the exchange with Stefano only a few minutes ago, Jana smiled rather wryly and shook her head. 'But not so irresistible that he doesn't quite happily take someone else out to lunch in my place if I'm not available,' she reminded him. 'I hardly think Stefano would miss me if I went home tomorrow!'

Marco said something in his own tongue, short and evidently virulent, and she wondered if she had the nerve to ask him what it was, but he was frowning so fiercely that she took a sip from her wine glass instead and decided that, for the moment, the subject of Stefano was better left alone.

Obviously Marco expected her to be upset by Stefano's inconstancy, and she could not bring herself at the moment to let him know how little in fact it bothered her. Stefano was charming and attractive, but he was simply not important enough in her life for her to let his fickleness upset her. It had been Marco, she remembered, who had forecast so confidently how much of a distraction his young cousin was likely to prove for her, and he would find it hard to believe that she had not been swept off her feet.

It was several moments before it struck her that Marco's words about Stefano finding her irresistible because, as a Venetian, he was a lover of beautiful things, applied equally as much to Marco himself, and her heart thudded hard as she glanced at the sternly handsome face opposite. Strong fingers curled about hers and he looked across and smiled curiously, as if he suspected she was day-dreaming, the touch of his hand bringing her back to awareness.

But Marco never gave her cause to think that he saw her as anything other than the niece of his old friend. His fingers squeezed hers, very gently—well, almost never.

CHAPTER SIX

STEFANO was angry, although he had done his best to pretend that all he felt was disappointment because Jana had once more turned down an invitation to have lunch with him. That was no doubt why he had not come out to join them, but had gone off somewhere on his own. As far as Jana was aware no one had yet made any mention of his unexpected appearance at the restaurant yesterday, when she was lunching with Marco, and personally she saw no reason for explanations; she had refused his invitation, so he was therefore quite entitled to take someone else in her place.

They had finished breakfast some time before, and Marco had retired to the smaller *sala* with her uncle, probably to discuss the material collected yesterday. They had long and sometimes very animated discussions on every aspect of the project, and sometimes they disagreed, although their differences of opinion were never malicious. Usually it was Marco who eventually yielded to Giles' age and experience even though, Jana suspected, he was not always convinced.

Signora Abrizzi sat on the terrace balcony reading the morning papers, while Jana occupied another chair nearby and gazed out at the now familiar skyline of Venice, enthralled as ever by the view. She liked sitting out there in the mornings when it was still fairly cool, and she was unaware of the small sigh of contentment that escaped her until the Signora lowered her newspaper and smiled.

'You like it out here, Jana?'

Willing to admit her complete enchantment with almost everything about Venice, Jana turned and smiled. 'It's beautiful! It always reminds me of a Canaletto—a whole series of Canalettos, in fact, because every time I turn my head, there's a different picture to look at!' A little diffident about her adulation, she laughed and shook her head. 'I can wax quite poetic,' she confessed. 'Venice seems to have the knack of turning ordinary daylight into such wonderful shimmering colours, and the overall effect is—breathtaking!'

'Ah, you are becoming an adopted Venetian, eh, *cara*?' Obviously the idea met with her approval, for the Signora smiled still. 'That is good! I miss Venice when I am away, but always when I come back I feel that I have become more attached to her because of my absence—it is a good feeling.'

'I can believe you.' Jana glanced across at the balustrade that surrounded the balcony terrace, below which the Vincella Eagle hovered. By going to the edge of the balcony, she could see it at much closer quarters, but it was no less grim and menacing from above than seen from the courtyard below—it still made her shudder. 'And the Eagle of the Vincella watches over it all like a—like a sentry. It must be a wonderful feeling to belong to something like this, *signora*. I envy you.'

'Ah, *sì*, *l'Aquila*!' Francesca put down her newspaper; apparently she much preferred to talk, especially to such an interested listener. 'He has hovered there for hundreds of years; the symbol of the power of the Vincella, though that kind of power is much diminished now.' Her smile might have indicated that she felt regret for the dwindled powers of her family, but it was difficult to be sure. 'In the modern world there is little room for such men as the old Vincella, eh, Jana?'

It was an interesting point, and Jana took a moment to think about it. 'I'm not so sure that the same power doesn't exist still, *signora*, but it takes a different form, there are men just as ruthless still, but they're more discreet about what they do.' She laughed when she realised how weighty the statement sounded. 'That isn't meant to be as profound as it sounds, but I'm sure you know what I mean.'

'*Sì, sì*, I know what you mean.' The Signora leaned back in her chair, relaxed and with her heavy-lidded eyes half closed against the increasing brightness of the sun as it crept around the shadow of the *palazzo* and dazzled them. 'The Vincella have a long history, Jana, and most of it seems to be somehow connected with *l'Aquila* and its influence.'

'Marco told me about the original one, the one that one of the popes gave to the first Vincella.'

'Ah!' Obviously she found that a little surprising, but she said no more at the moment about it. 'There have been a great many intrigues during the history of this *palazzo*, Jana, but a great many generations have come and gone. There have been great loves, important marriages, and some tragedies, but always *l'Aquila* has watched over the Vincella—the family prospers while he guards us. It is the old legend.'

'I didn't know about that.' Jana wondered why Marco had omitted it from his version of the old story unless, despite his appearance of practicality, he was in some way affected by the old legend.

The Signora cast her an almost sly look from her expressive dark eyes and half-smiled. 'Did Marco not tell you that?'

'No, he didn't.'

Jana leaned back her head and gazed lazily at the view of soaring roof-tops and hazy blue sky through half-closed eyes, remembering Marco's dilemma over the sale of the Eagle, and she wondered what Francesca would have to say about that if she knew. Not that she believed in fairy-stories herself, of course, but she must try if she could to dissuade him from parting with it; although she doubted if she had that much influence with him. Just thinking about persuading him, however, was disturbing enough and she sought hastily to dismiss the prospect from her mind.

'I could stay out here all day,' she remarked, and the Signora nodded. The subject was changed and the disturbing problem deferred for the time being. 'It's so peaceful!'

She contemplated her surroundings with a lazy eye. Stone urns stood all around the terrace, filled with flowering vines and bright red geraniums that tumbled over the edge of their containers, muskily spicy on the warm morning air. Roses too, although crowded into corners and neglected, nevertheless bloomed in profusion, red and yellow heads hanging low as the sun became hotter, and scattering soft scented petals on the stone paving, fluttering with every light breeze that stirred.

Access to the terrace from the main *sala*, a room the size of a ballroom in Jana's opinion, was via a pair of impressively tall glass doors, and it never failed to set her imagination working when she saw them stood wide open as they were now. In her mind's eye she saw the rooms beyond them bright with lights and noisy with laughter and music; and occasionally the shadowy figure of some past member of the powerful Vincella drifting out on to this same balcony with a lover, to look at the city by moonlight. It was a fanciful indulgence, but one which she frequently enjoyed when she sat out there.

Giles too, liked to sit out, and he had spent quite a lot of time out there since he came from hospital, absorbing the sun that was so necessary to his recovery and resting, but at the same time pursuing his project by editing the notes that Jana typed for him each day. She had noticed too that lately Signora Abrizzi had taken to sharing both his task and his company, a situation that was not without its element of surprise, for Giles was not a man to form hasty friendships.

It was fairly obvious too, that Francesca Abrizzi did not sit with him simply because she felt sorry for a man recovering from an illness, for she so evidently enjoyed herself. They discussed the project and checked notes; the Signora even made suggestions on occasion that were incorporated into the book. She was a charming and intelligent woman, of course, but it was so unusual for Giles to be persuaded out of his customary reserve by a comparative stranger that Jana could not help wondering if the air of Venice had not worked some kind of miracle for her rather shy uncle.

If Stefano had noticed anything he had not so far said anything, but then Jana suspected that Stefano did not pay much attention to anything that did not immediately concern him personally. She looked at him now as he came out on to the balcony, still wearing a trace of his earlier sulky look, and flopped into the chair next to hers, his long legs crossed one over the other and one hand supporting his chin.

The Signora caught Jana's eye briefly and she pulled a face behind her son's back. Then she got to her feet and ruffled his black hair affectionately, stroking a hand over his face and under his chin briefly as she smiled down at him. '*Cosa c'è, caro*, eh?'

Stefano glanced across at Jana, then shrugged carelessly. 'Nothing is the matter, Mamma, *grazie*.'

'*Bene!*' She bent her head and kissed his brow, then once more caught Jana's eye and smiled. 'I will go over there and read my newspaper, so that you may talk with Jana and not interrupt my reading—*d'accordo*?'

It was an obvious move, but inevitable, Jana recognised, and she had no real objection to being left with Stefano, for his moods seldom lasted very long. She watched him from the corner of her eye as the Signora moved across out of earshot, and settled down once more with the morning papers.

He most often wore white or cream suits because they made the most flattering contrast to his smooth dark complexion, she suspected, and his shirts were usually light blue or brown. This morning he was wearing a cream suit with a brown silk shirt, and he knew just how stunningly handsome he looked, Jana had no doubt. Stefano suffered from no degree of false modesty—he enjoyed the effect he had on the opposite sex and made no secret of it. Nor could Jana find it in her heart to blame him for there was a curious suggestion of vulnerability about him for all his air of confidence.

Getting his own way was something he expected as his right, and he did not get it as often as he would like where Jana was concerned, so that his faintly sulky anger was probably an expression of his uncertainty. At the moment his lashes concealed the look in his eyes, but his mouth was pursed in dislike of her latest refusal to accompany him rather than work on her uncle's project.

'How can I be blamed for taking another woman to lunch when you will not come with me?' he asked, when she had once more shaken her head at him, and he used his free hand to emphasise his complaint.

Jana looked at him curiously. 'Have I blamed you for taking someone else to lunch?' she asked, only a little wary of his histrionics, and Stefano frowned.

'Have you not?' he countered. 'You are naturally angry —hurt because I arrived with another woman to lunch at your favourite restaurant——'

'Oh, that!'

'It was very hurtful to you, hah?' He gave her no time to deny it, but hurried on, intent on impressing her with his regret. 'For that I am very sorry, Jana; but I also was hurt to discover you there with Marco. Perhaps you too should be sorry.'

Jana felt the whole thing was rather a storm in a tea-cup, and she saw no reason at all why she should apologise for having lunch with Marco. 'I told you I couldn't come with you because I was working, Stefano, and it was true. We'd had a very hot and very busy morning and Marco gave me lunch because—well, because it was quicker than coming back here, that's all.'

It wasn't all, she knew, but she saw no reason to tell Stefano exactly what had led to Marco's taking her to lunch at Il Giardino. 'At your favourite restaurant, eh?' Stefano demanded, and she sighed.

'Marco knows I like Il Giardino and that's why he took me there, I expect, but I didn't know I was going and it wasn't the reason I turned down your invitation, Stefano. If I hadn't been so busy I'd have loved to go with you.'

'Poor Jana, it is not the same with Marco—you were disappointed, eh, *carissima*?' He had absolutely no doubt that she had been bitterly disappointed at having to make do with his cousin for company, and at the moment Jana saw no way of telling him the truth without being far more unfeeling than she cared to be. Reaching over, he squeezed her fingers consolingly. 'But if you come with me today, *bella mia*, it will perhaps make up for your disappointment. We will take a ride in a gondola, which is what you like best, eh? And I will give you lunch at La Falcone, which you will like better than Il Giardino, I promise.'

Lunch at one of the most expensive restaurants in Venice was admittedly a temptation, and just for once it would probably be worth missing a day's work for. But it did not rest entirely with her, she felt, for there was Marco and her uncle to be considered whenever she took time off from the project.

There were no two ways about it, she would enjoy it enormously, gliding along in a gondola with Stefano, for he was just the kind of man to be with in that most romantic form of transport. But outings such as Stefano had in mind were for people with nothing to do but enjoy themselves, and she did have other things to do. Things that Marco was putting himself out to help with.

'It sounds wonderful, Stefano, but dare I take time off? Marco is giving his time to helping while Giles is ill, and I really feel I should consider him.'

'*Dannazione!*' Stefano declared with such violence that the Signora in her corner of the terrace, looked up briefly and flicked an enquiring brow in their direction. He leaned forward in his chair, using his hands to express his frustration, his feet planted squarely on the stone paving as he looked at her with dark glittering eyes. 'How can I not take other women to lunch when you will not take time from your—your scribbling to come with me? Tell me that! You tell me, hah?' He flung out his hands in a gesture of despair, then flopped back in his chair again, supporting his head on one hand while he glared at her reproachfully. 'Marco does wrong to blame me for—for flaunting Nena Vadrini before you at your favourite restaurant!'

'Marco?' Jana stared at him for a moment, wondering if she could have heard him right. 'Are you sure *Marco* said that?'

'Who else? He thinks I do it to—how is it?—show off! He says that he told Mama the evening before that he meant to take you to Il Giardino for lunch, and that I was there when he did so, but I do not remember!'

It was probably true, Jana mused a little dazedly. It was like Stefano to hear something and not take notice of it unless it directly concerned himself; he had probably been busy laying his own plans at the time. But she could not imagine why Marco had not enlightened her when she mentioned Lucio's behaving as if he expected them; unless he preferred her to think that he had acted on the spur of the moment.

'You know I would not behave like that, *carissima*!' Stefano was still intent of impressing her with his own position. 'Marco—hah! He is trying too much to be like your uncle; too much the protector!'

It could be the truth, Jana realised with a start, and found the idea strangely unwelcome, so that she frowned over it, then shook her head. 'I hardly think so, Stefano.'

'But he blames me that I do not sit at home and— mope?—because you cannot come with me!'

Knowing how prone he was to exaggeration, Jana shook her head. She could not see Marco being quite so concerned with the tenderness of her feelings. 'Oh, Stefano, he didn't say *that*, surely!'

'He intends that!' Stefano insisted firmly. 'I know! He was angry because I did not simply sit at home and mourn the fact that you cannot come with me because he forces you to work with him!'

'But I'm not forced to go with him, Stefano, you do exaggerate so! Now please can't we drop the subject?'

'You understand that I would rather have taken you, Jana, that I took Nena Vadrini only because you refused to come with me?'

'Yes, of course I understand; but I still don't think I should desert Marco this morning. He won't like it with so much to do.'

'But there is plenty of time to do these notes that you do,' he insisted, spotting a weakening chink in her resistance. 'You will not leave Venice until after the ball, will you? And there are several weeks until that happens.'

'No. No, I suppose we won't be going until after that;

I'd forgotten all about the ball.' She sought a change of subject eagerly. 'I'm quite excited about that—have you decided on your costume yet?'

'I wait only to learn what you will wear and then I shall decide.'

She remembered how they had gone through all this before, and she laughed and shook her head. 'And I've told you I'm keeping it a secret until the night!'

His dark persuasive eyes speculated for a second or two, then he shrugged carelessly and leaned towards her once more. '*Benissimo, bella mia,* but I will have an answer for today! You will come with me, eh? *Per piacere,* Jana!'

The idea of a gondola ride and an expensive lunch was a temptation in itself, but added to the dark persuasion in Stefano's eyes it was irresistible, and she sighed as she got to her feet. 'I'll see Marco,' she decided, smiling obliquely. 'I'll tell him—I'll ask him if he minds my skipping the schedule for today, so that I can have lunch with you.'

Stefano left his chair swiftly, his smile beaming, satisfied as a sleek handsome cat now that he had his way, and he reached for her hand and squeezed it. Drawing her to his side, he looked down into her face with bright gleaming eyes, his voice pitched low although there was little likelihood of his mother overhearing.

'Do not concern yourself, *carissima,* I will tell Marco that you are to come with me!' He shrugged and spread one hand wide as he smiled down at her, cock-a-hoop at having his own way. 'He cannot complain after all, when he has said that you are hurt by my taking other women out in your place—it is his fault for making you work so hard! What better way to mend the hurt, *cara mia,* than to give you a whole day in my company, eh? I will tell him!'

'No, Stefano, please!' She freed her hand and tried not to look at him while she explained. 'I don't like delegating jobs like that; I'll see Marco myself and ask him, I'd much rather.'

Obviously he did not understand her at all, but eventually he heaved his shoulders in a resigned shrug and bent to kiss her mouth lightly before he let her go. '*Bene*, as you wish—I will remain here until you are ready.'

Signora Abrizzi looked up as Jana approached her chair and smiled, her dark eyes faintly curious, so that Jana paused to explain as briefly as she could, that Stefano had, after all, managed to persuade her. Not that she would be in the least surprised, but she would be pleased, Jana thought.

'I'm going to ask for the day off,' she said, glancing across at Stefano as he flopped once more on to the cane lounging chair and took out a cigarette. 'Stefano had something in mind and wants me to have a day out with him.'

'Ah, *bene*!' There was no doubt that his mother was as pleased as Stefano himself, and she reached out and took Jana's hand for a moment. 'It is good that you go with Stefi and have fun, *cara*, you work so hard on those endless notes! You are young and lovely and you should enjoy yourself more—I have said so to Giles!'

It did not really surprise her to hear it, and Jana smiled. 'Oh, Giles isn't a slave-driver, *signora*,' she told her, and noticed the older woman's faintly puzzled frown.

'Ah, *si*, I understand!' she said before Jana could explain. 'No, no, I do not think this of Giles, but perhaps Marco is the slave-driver, hah?'

'Oh no, not at all!'

Jana was hasty in her denial and the Signora recognised it with a swift arch of her fine brows; a gesture that brought a faint flush of colour to Jana's cheeks so that she hastily lowered her head for a moment, concealing the unexpected blush with the sweep of her golden hair.

'You think not?' Signora Abrizzi enquired gently.

'Marco's only anxious to get as much done as possible for Giles' sake, Signora Abrizzi.'

'Ah, *sì, mia cara*, Marco has the warm heart for all he has the look of the tyrant, eh? You have found this?'

It wasn't easy to answer such a question with the Signora's dark eyes on her, so instead Jana shrugged lightly and smiled. 'I find him very easy to work with, we get along well together, considering.'

'Considering that he is the man he is and that you are not perhaps so—amenable as he would always like, eh, *cara*?'

'Something like that, though I have been known to rebel on occasion.' She caught Stefano's eye on her, and noticed a shadow of a frown between his brows. Stefano did not like being kept waiting. 'I think I'd better go and see Marco and ask him if it's all right for me to skip my note-taking this morning, if you'll excuse me, Signora Abrizzi.'

'Jana.' The Signora smiled. 'I would like very much for you to call me by my name, if you please. Francesca, hah?'

Only too willing to comply, Jana nodded and smiled. 'Yes, of course, I'd like to, *sig*—Francesca.'

'*Bene!*' She sat back comfortably, evidently prepared to talk on, no matter how impatient her son became. 'Where is it that Stefi is taking you?' Without waiting for a reply she hurried on. 'You much admire our Venetian glass, do you not? Perhaps you would like to see where it is made?'

'Oh, Murano, the island where it's all made! I know of it, of course.'

'That is right. They have been making glass there for almost seven hundred years and it is the most exquisite glass in the world without doubt, you will agree? But——' she wagged a warning finger, 'if you should wish to buy do not do so from the factory itself, for it is much more expensive than to buy from the shops here. Very difficult to believe, is it not? But it is so, Jana, so remember that, eh?'

'I will, I promise!' She glanced across once more in Stefano's direction and pulled a face. 'I'd enjoy it enormously, but Stefano's already made plans, I believe. We're going for a gondola ride and then having lunch at La Falcone.'

'Ah *sì*, much more *romantico*!' Francesca laughed and rolled her eyes. 'And much more to Stefano's liking, eh? But now I think you *must* go, *cara*, for Stefano is getting very impatient!'

She was right, Jana thought; he was looking across at her with an unmistakable frown and she pulled a face. 'Stefano isn't the most patient man on earth, is he?'

'No, *cara*, but that is flattering, *no*?' She looked up and smiled, speculating on just how flattered she was, Jana thought, and felt slightly out of her depth for a moment.

'I'd better go and find Marco and see if he minds me having the day off, before Stefano gets too impatient and sees him himself.'

Francesca regarded her steadily for a moment. 'Would Marco tell you that he minded, Jana, do you think?' she asked.

Rather than answer Jana laughed and shook back her hair as she hurried off to find Marco and discover whether or not he minded her going. She had never considered what she would actually do if he did, but Francesca's rather enigmatic question had given her cause to think about it, and she hoped she never had to find out.

Expecting to find Giles and Marco together in the smaller *sala* where she had left them earlier, she found instead that Marco was alone and he looked up quickly when she came in. A brief glance was enough to tell her that he was ready to go out for their usual daily round, and she carefully avoided his eyes when she realised it.

Casually dressed, as he always was for their excursions, he looked cool and elegant in pale grey slacks and a blue shirt that contrasted flatteringly with his olive-dark skin and black hair, and she felt a sudden and inexplicable reluctance to tell him that she had decided not to go with him. He came straight to the point when he saw her and took her by surprise.

'Ah, Jana! I have been discussing with Giles the idea of showing you the Eagle of the Vincella. You still wish to see it, do you not?'

Jana's heart gave a sudden and unexpected lurch and she gazed at him for a moment, scarcely believing that he was actually going to show her that wonderful, mythical creature that symbolised his family's pride and, if Francesca was to be believed, their fortunes. 'Oh yes, please, Marco! Francesca's just been telling me how it has always been regarded as a kind of guardian of your family's good luck, and I'm dying to see it; to know that it really exists!'

'But of course it exists, *piccina*! Have I not told you that it does?'

'Yes, of course, but——'

'But seeing is believing; is that not your saying?'

Catching a glimpse of amusement in his eyes for a moment, she pursed her mouth reproachfully, looking up at him through her lashes. 'I know you probably think I'm horribly naïve for getting so excited about it,' she told him, 'but I can't help it, Marco. I find it incredibly exciting to think of the Eagle being in your family for more than three hundred years—it *is* exciting!'

'Yes, of course it is, and I promise that I was not laughing at you.' He regarded her for a moment in more serious vein, she thought. 'Have you spoken about the Eagle to Stefano?' he asked, and she shook her head instinctively.

'No. Except to say that you promised to show it to me.' It occurred to her then what he might have in mind and she frowned her dislike of his not trusting her. 'And I haven't said anything to *anyone* about you selling the Eagle,' she told him, adding hastily, 'except to Giles, and I made him promise not to let it go any further, or even say anything to you about it.' She slid the tip of her tongue across her lips, suddenly conscious of the trust he had placed in her by confiding in her as he had. 'I know you told me in confidence, Marco, but I haven't given you away—I wouldn't.'

Slowly the dark eyes traversed her flushed face and he smiled after a moment. 'No, I do not believe you would, *piccina*, otherwise I would not have told you.'

'I'm sorry about Giles, but I thought it was possible you'd confided in him too; I didn't know——'

'That you were my sole confidante?' A sardonic smile curved his wide mouth for a moment. 'I am not often so ready to share my innermost thoughts, Jana, you are to be congratulated on breaking down my usually firm barriers, *piccola*!'

Feeling slightly light-headed, Jana avoided his eyes once more and kept her mind on the fact that she was at last to see the golden eagle about whose fate he was presumably still undecided. 'When can I see the Eagle?' she asked, and he laughed softly at her seeming impatience.

'Tonight, after we have had dinner.'

'I can't wait!' she laughed herself now, at her own enthusiasm and shook her head when she saw his smile. 'All right, I *am* naïve about things like the Eagle, but you and Giles are so much more—more acclimatised to things like that than I am. I find it much too exciting to simply accept it as you do.'

She had come quite close while they talked and Marco reached out suddenly and touched her cheek, showing a curious gentleness that always surprised her, although she had experienced it often enough now to accept it as part of his make-up. Long fingers curved about her cheek and his dark eyes studied her for a second before he smiled.

'It is not naïve, Jana; or if it is then naïveté is very

attractive and desirable.' His hand stroked across her cheek and was then withdrawn quite suddenly, and he looked down at her with a hint of enquiry, pushing both hands into the pockets of his slacks. 'Did you come to find me because you are ready to leave?'

Brought rather suddenly back to earth, Jana had to make an effort to recall her errand. 'I wanted to ask you if you'd mind me not coming with you today.'

'You wish to go somewhere with Stefano? To make up for yesterday?'

He would know it was Stefano, of course, but she was puzzled by her own lack of enthusiasm for the idea of spending a whole day just enjoying herself with Stefano; and she had no doubt that she would enjoy herself. 'He's thinking of taking a gondola ride and then having lunch at La Falcone, so he said.'

'La Falcone?' His eyes glittered with amusement, and she wondered if he often found his more flamboyant young cousin a source of amusement. 'Have you never been there before, Jana?'

'No, never. I'm looking forward to it.'

'And to the gondola ride also, I expect, eh?'

There was something about him that was curiously different, and she could not decide what it was, only that it made her uneasy. 'I thought you wouldn't mind, Marco.' She glanced down at her plain linen dress and laughed. 'I'd better put on something a bit more grand for La Falcone, I suppose, hadn't I?'

'Of course you must go with him, if that is what you wish to do,' Marco said quietly. 'Enjoy yourself, *piccina*, eh?'

His smile when she looked up at him suggested that he knew just how much she wanted to go with Stefano, and she felt an almost irresistible desire to tell him that she was not half so swept off her feet by the prospect as he seemed to think, although she could not pretend she was not going to enjoy it either. In the circumstances she said nothing, but smiled her thanks and turned to go.

'You would look very grand in the pink dress that you have, with the long sleeves, Jana. Why do you not wear that one, eh?'

It had not even occurred to her before that he noticed what she wore, although Stefano was obviously the type of man who would always know what a woman was wearing, and probably which perfume she used too. She almost voiced her surprise, but thought better of it, and merely smiled instead as she turned away once more.

'Then I'll wear that one,' she said as she walked across to the door. 'Stefano's sure to like it!'

A murmur of laughter followed her and she turned to look at him again, her eyes faintly suspicious. Marco was shaking his head, his eyes a fathomless dark glow between thick lashes. 'Do you not know that Stefano would like whatever you wear, *dolce mia*? He is young and *romantico* and you are a very lovely girl; how could he not like any dress that you choose to wear for him, eh, Jana?'

'Any dress *you* choose, as it happens!' she reminded him with a slight edge on her voice, and she wondered why it was that she so resented him choosing what was possibly her most flattering dress because he knew it would please his cousin.

'*Sì, piccina*, a dress that I choose because I know that it becomes you, and you wish to please Stefano,' he agreed in a quiet voice, and his slightly narrowed eyes regarded her for a moment steadily. 'Do you not like me to remark upon which dress suits you well, Jana? Does it—offend you?'

'Offend——?' She stared at him for a moment, then shook her head, determinedly bringing her voice under control. 'Oh no, Marco, I'm not offended. I'm grateful that you take the trouble to help me look as good as possible for Stefano—thank you!' She closed the door quickly behind

her, but not before she heard a murmured word in Italian
that she felt sure was surprise, and her legs felt oddly unsteady as she made her way to her room.

The deep pink dress was every bit as successful as Marco
had forecast it would be, and Stefano had scarcely taken his
eyes off her all the while they were in the gondola that took
them slowly past palaces and churches, crowded together at
the water's edge, seemingly balanced on the very edge of
the *fondamente* on which they were built. Venice always
turned her best face to the water, and the very best way to
see it was from a gondola. Jana felt she was being thoroughly spoiled when, after leaving the restaurant, they took
another gondola and she sat curled up in the curve at Stefano's arm contentedly watching the passing scene.

'You enjoyed La Falcone?'

His voice sounded deep and soft close to her ear and the
murmur of his breath tickled her neck, so that it made it
rather difficult for her to think clearly about her opinion of
the baroque palace he had taken her to for lunch. Certainly
it had been impressive and it was almost surely far more
expensive than Il Giardino, but she could not quite bring
herself to tell him that the simpler place had been more to
her taste. Instead she smiled up at him and nodded.

'I was very impressed,' she told him, which was in no
way an untruth.

Perhaps it was something in her voice that gave him a
clue, or it could have been that Stefano was far more
shrewd than most people guessed; his mother claimed he
was a clever businessman when he put his mind to it.
Whatever it was he slid a finger beneath her chin and
turned her face up to him, looking down at her with bright
quizzical eyes for a second or two before he said anything.

'But you still prefer Il Giardino, hah?' he demanded,

and snorted his disgust without giving her time to reply. 'And perhaps with Marco, eh?'

'Stefano, please don't——'

'Oh, *carissima mia*! I tease you, hah?' He kissed her so unexpectedly that she was unprepared for it and struggled for a moment against his hold on her, only slowly yielding to the irresistible pressure of his mouth on hers when she realised how enjoyable the sensation was. He raised his head and his mouth hovered just above hers while he looked down into her eyes, then he smiled. 'Of course you prefer to be with me—I am teasing you, Jana, eh?'

He would never even think that she wanted to be with anyone else, Jana realised a little dazedly. Stefano was a practised charmer, and he had no illusions about his own abilities; it was doubtful if he ever thought about his cousin being any kind of competition, and yet Jana realised as she eased herself slightly away from him that she could recall Marco's light, gentle kiss as they stood in the Querini gallery with incredible clarity, even now.

It was a disturbing thought to suddenly bring to mind at a moment like this, but though her mouth still tingled from Stefano's kiss, she had not been so completely swept away by the experience that she lost sight of other moments. Stefano kissed her once more, lightly on the side of her neck, and tightened his arm about her so that she was drawn closer with little option but to press still nearer to him.

'Tomorrow you will come with me again, Jana, *eh*?' His voice was low and infinitely persuasive, close to her ear, his breath wafting warmly against her skin and arousing sensations she could do little to subdue. 'You will not refuse me, *carissima*, I know you will not; not when we have enjoyed this so very much.' He kissed her ear and pressed his face into the soft silkiness of her hair, sighing deeply when he put both arms around her and held her close against him. *'Faccia pure, mia bella* Jana; please come.'

Tempted, no matter how she steeled herself against it, Jana shook her head. 'I'll have to see, Stefano—I doubt it very much.'

'But you wish to, hah?' He gave her no opportunity to reply, but leaned over her and pressed his mouth to hers, heedless of the fact that it was broad daylight and that they were in full view of people passing by. His eyes had a bright determined gleam and he breathed his words against her ear, lyrical Italian words that she could not understand, but which needed little translation, and after a while he raised his head and looked at her, held close to his chest. 'I will persuade you, *carissima*. I am very good at persuading, you will see!'

Jana, who had no doubt he was good at persuading, wondered how firm she could be when it came to the point. Stefano was bent on persuading her, and she knew in her heart that Giles would not blame her if she really wanted to spend a few days with Stefano. Looking up into that handsome, confident face, she could not resist a smile, and Stefano kissed her once more.

'You wish to be persuaded, eh, *carissima mia?*' His mouth lightly touched her neck, and his voice was low, so low that even she barely heard it. '*Bella mia* Jana, you will not refuse me, eh? *Carissima?* You will come with me?'

'Stefano——'

Her protest was only half-hearted, and Stefano's kiss put a determined stop to it before she could get beyond his own name. Her head was spinning and she could do nothing about the excitement of being in his arms, and being kissed as she had seldom been kissed before. Almost without realising it she nodded her head slowly when he whispered a suggestion that they go on forever in their gondola.

'Jana!' He kissed her again, and held her close. '*Bella mia.*'

There had seemed no reason why they should not stay out for dinner too and they had gone to a smaller place this time, because Stefano teased her with her taste for the less ostentatious restaurants. Jana drank a little too much wine, and danced, which she had not done for some time, and as they drove the last part of their journey home in a *motoscafo* that Stefano had insisted on hiring, Jana wondered when she had ever had a more eventful day.

She was tired, but she felt a pleasant glow of happiness that was not entirely due to her companion, as the looming darkness of the Palazzo Vincella came into view and the *motoscafo* drew up at the landing stage. Lights streamed out from several windows, and like all the other *palazzi* in Venice, it seemed to float on the water, much less grim and menacing in its night-time garb of lights than in the daytime.

Stefano helped her from the boat, and paid off the driver, and Jana picked her way across the treacherous surface of the courtyard with his hand helping her, wondering at her memory for certain bad spots that could trip the unwary and cause a fall.

The low archway admitted them to the courtyard proper, and it was instinctive to glance up at the looming figure of the Eagle above the portico, looking more menacing than ever in the semi-darkness, with the helpless stone man gripped in its unrelenting claws. Then she stopped suddenly, staring up at the Eagle, her breath caught in her throat a hand to her mouth as she stared upward.

'Jana! What is wrong?'

He too looked up at the craggy stone eagle lowering above them and shrugged. But the sight of it reminded Jana of a promise Marco had made her that morning, just before she left with Stefano. 'Tonight, when we have had dinner,' he had promised, and she had blamed him for laughing at her obvious excitement.

Stefano was holding her arm firmly, curious and a little impatient when she continued to stare up at the Eagle instead of answering. 'I do not understand you, Jana, what is the matter?'

'The Eagle.' Her voice was husky, and she was appalled to find herself almost tearful as she looked at him at last and shook her head. 'Oh, Stefano, how am I going to face him? Marco promised to show me the Eagle of the Vincella after dinner tonight, and I forgot about it!'

Obviously puzzled by her taking it so seriously, Stefano shrugged.

'There will be other times,' he told her carelessly. 'It is not so important, *carissima*, surely that you look so—upset.'

'But it *is*—you don't understand, Stefano!' He took her arm and together they entered that vast, impressive hall, their footsteps echoing back at them from the towering walls and the curving staircase. 'He promised because I was so anxious to see it, don't you see? He was showing it to me as a special favour and I—I forgot.'

Stefano started to say something, but a door opened as they reached the gallery, and Marco came out from the *sala*. It was very late and she doubted if her uncle was still up; Francesca too had probably gone to bed, and the house had a curiously listening atmosphere that made Jana shiver and press just a little closer to Stefano.

'Marco.' He spoke to his cousin with a slight air of wariness, and then glanced down at Jana's unhappy face. 'We have been to dinner and for a gondola ride, and Jana has enjoyed herself, have you not, *carissima*?'

'Yes, very much.' She licked her lips anxiously, unable to take her eyes from Marco's dark unfathomable face, the eyes half hidden by thick lashes. 'Stefano, will you—will you let me speak to Marco on my own for a few minutes, please?'

Disliking the idea intensely, Stefano was not slow to say so, and he frowned at his cousin. 'You do not have to——'

'Please, Stefano!'

She interrupted him sharply, her voice thin and unsteady, and Marco neither spoke nor moved, but stayed just outside the door of the *sala*. Even Stefano had to recognise the intensity of her feelings at the moment, and after a second or two, he shrugged. Bending his head, he kissed her mouth boldly, almost as if he defied his cousin to deny him the privilege.

'*Bene, carissima*, I will leave you. *Buona notte!* Marco— *buona notte!*'

Marco murmured a reply, then turned and walked back into the *sala*, leaving Jana to follow on legs that felt suddenly scarcely able to hold her weight. She found him standing over near the window looking out at the bright mass of light that was Venice at night, and standing with his back to her.

'Marco, I'm sorry.'

There seemed nothing else to say and she could almost feel the tension in him, see the tautness in the long hands that were clasped together behind him. He didn't turn and his voice had a flat, hard edge that made her shake her head. 'You are entitled to go out and enjoy yourself, Jana. You are in no way obliged to answer to me.'

'But you know I wanted to see the Eagle!'

'I had thought so, that is why I removed it from its place of safety and brought it up here, but it seems you had other—amusements, more important!' He half turned and the dark eyes glittered at her like chips of jet between their thick lashes. 'Were Stefano's kisses so irresistible that you could not remember anything else?'

'Please, Marco!'

'He has made progress, I think!' He turned right around to face her now and she found it very hard to meet his eyes. 'He has the air of one who is in a position to do as he pleases! Who has made a conquest—am I not right, Jana?'

He was angry, but somehow she did not quite believe it was simply because she had failed to see the Eagle when he had brought it out for her; there was something else, something that made him glitter and burn with anger. His strong features looked cruel as she had never seen them look, and there was such a burning intensity in his eyes that she shivered as she looked at him.

'Are his kisses so heady that you can forget everything else when he kisses you? Are they, Jana?'

She was trembling and her cheeks were flushed as she tried to look directly at him. He had no right to talk to her as he was, and yet she seemed unable to do anything to stop him. Clenching her hands tightly, she managed at last to look at him and her head was pounding as she spoke, her voice shivery and uncertain.

'Stefano kissed me,' she said huskily. 'Several times, and I suppose it was that that was partly responsible for me forgetting about your promise to show me the Eagle, but it wasn't only that, Marco, I swear it wasn't.'

'Do you expect me to believe that?'

'Does it matter if you don't?'

Her response was less defiant than defensive, and she sounded as breathless as if she had run a very long way. Her breathing was short and erratic and she was unable to control it, and her legs trembled so that she felt barely able to stand. She almost fell into his arms when Marco reached out and pulled her against him with bruising force, knocking the breath from her and smothering her small cry of surprise with the fierce hardness of his mouth.

Pressed so close that she could feel every taut muscle in

his body, she clung to him helplessly for a second or two, not even knowing what she did, her arms around his neck and her fingers in the thick blackness of his hair. But it was anger that fired his passion and her own senses recognised it and were frightened by it, so that she struggled against him after a moment or two and broke away.

His hands still at her waist, she stared up into his face, scarcely recognising the harsh passionate features that looked down at her; the hard mouth and burning black eyes that seemed to see right through her. Then she turned swiftly, pulling herself free, and almost ran to the door, hearing the faint sound of her name as she opened it and fled along the carpeted gallery to her room.

Stefano had made her forget about the Eagle of the Vincella, but Marco's kiss could make her forget everything and everybody, even Stefano, and for a while she sat in her room trembling and uncertain, trying to restore her emotions to a level of sanity, and wondering where she could possibly go from there.

CHAPTER SEVEN

To Jana the prospect of breakfast the following morning promised to be something of an ordeal, for she could hardly think that everything would be exactly the same after the way Marco had received her last night. The whole day with Stefano, his kisses and his flattering attentiveness, were pushed somewhere to the back of her mind, but those few minutes with Marco still lingered with startling clarity and refused to be forgotten, and she found the fact not only disturbing but vaguely alarming somehow.

She was in two minds when she first got up whether or not to wait and go in to breakfast with Giles, but on reflection it seemed such a childish manoeuvre that she abandoned it almost at once. The reflection in her bedroom mirror showed a slightly apprehensive face with blue eyes that were if anything a slightly darker shade this morning than usual, their colour in part deepened by the dark blue dress she was wearing; a dress that also showed up the brightness of her hair and added a kind of translucency to her fair skin.

Seeing herself reflected against the background of an ornately baroque bedroom always gave her a sense of unreality at first glance, and each time she half expected to wake up and find herself back in Giles' shabby Victorian villa in England. Such a richly ornate setting had at first made her feel curiously alien, but she enjoyed the comfort and luxury it offered, and lately she had begun to feel quite at home there. It was the possibility of those few dramatic moments with Marco changing things that troubled her.

Impatient suddenly with her own lack of confidence, she

shook back the silky thickness of her hair from her face in an unconscious gesture of defiance and turned from the mirror. She had no need to feel so nervous, and shrinking like a schoolgirl from the memory of one kiss was not the behaviour of a self-possessed woman; she was making too much of it.

In the *sala* she found only Francesca and Marco, and she hastily thanked heaven that Marco was not there alone as she went to join them. They both sat at one end of the table and had so obviously been talking together quite seriously that the hastily exchanged glances that greeted her appearance told their own story. They fell suddenly silent too, which made her pause briefly as she came across the room, for the low-voiced conversation had ceased too abruptly to be natural, and she hesitated to intrude.

It was Francesca who noticed her hesitation, and she looked across and smiled encouragingly. 'Ah, Jana *mia cara, buon giorno*!'

'Good morning, Francesca.' Jana took the chair opposite to her, on Marco's left, and she glanced as she did so at his face, but it told her nothing. 'Good morning, Marco.'

There was a hint of bravado in the greeting and it sounded much more short and formal than she had intended it to, although she did not realise it, but when he looked up and caught her eye it set her pulse racing wildly so that she hastily looked away. Not by so much as a flicker of an eyelash did he betray any emotion, and his voice was as quiet and as perfectly modulated as it always was when he answered her formal greeting.

'*Buon giorno*, Jana.'

He did not call her '*piccina*' as he more usually did, she noticed, and she felt an undeniable sense of regret for his formality without for a moment realising that she had set the pattern for it herself. Francesca passed her the coffee and looked across to see that fresh rolls were being brought for her, acting in the capacity of hostess as she most often did.

'You enjoyed yourself yesterday, eh, Jana?' she asked.

It was instinctive, Jana found, to glance at Marco before she answered, although his expression was hardly encouraging. He had a strangely withdrawn air about him this morning that could possibly mean he was embarrassed, although she thought it unlikely, and she wished Francesca had left her curiosity about her day out until Marco wasn't there.

'I enjoyed it very much, Francesca, thank you.'

'Ah, *bene*, then you must go again soon, hmm?'

Jana was unwilling to commit herself to anything at the moment, especially with Marco sitting there, so she merely smiled. Nodding her thanks to the girl who brought her fresh rolls, she waited until she had departed once more before she said anything. 'It was a wonderful day, Francesca, but I'm afraid we were terribly late back; it was one o'clock this morning before we arrived home!'

Francesca shrugged carelessly. '*Ma ben inteso!*' she said, and flashed her cousin a dark-eyed challenge that suggested she knew all about how angry he had been last night. 'Young people enjoying themselves do not consider the passing of time! It is part of the fun of being young, is it not? And who will blame you?' She knew well enough who had blamed her, Jana thought ruefully, and once more glanced at Marco as Francesca went on, determined to make her point. 'Giles was not concerned for you because he knew that you were with Stefano, so who else is to say you may not stay out just as late as you wish to, eh, *cara*?'

It wasn't easy, knowing that Marco was listening, and Jana shook her head slowly. 'In this case it did matter, as it happened, Francesca, because I'd been promised I could see the Eagle of the Vincella after dinner last night and

I—well, the truth is that I simply forgot about it, though I can't imagine how I could!'

'Ah, but I know my son, *cara*, and I know that it would not be easy for any young woman to remember the passing of time when Stefano sets out to make her forget, eh?' Rolling her eyes meaningly, Francesca took another roll on to her plate, and she frowned at her cousin impatiently when he still did not join in. 'Marco has forgiven you for forgetting about *l'Aquila*, Jana, I promise you!'

Jana studied him briefly from the corner of her eye and was unconvinced. 'I'm not so sure,' she said.

He could have confirmed it, she thought, vaguely annoyed by his attitude, but instead it was Francesca who reached over and pressed her hand reassuringly, a gesture that Jana felt would have carried more conviction coming from Marco himself. She wasn't at all convinced that he shared Francesca's lighthearted view of her lapse of memory, especially in view of the violence of his reception last night.

Then she realised suddenly that he was looking at her, holding her gaze with that familiar disturbing steadiness, his eyes still showing a glimpse of the same dark passion she had seen there last night, and she hastily shifted her gaze when she remembered the bruising hardness of his mouth. She could almost imagine that her mouth still tingled this morning, and it was only with difficulty that she stopped herself putting a hand to her lips.

'Am I to apologise for last night, Jana?' he asked, then typically gave her no opportunity to answer. 'I regret that I allowed you to see me so angry, though I do not admit that I had no cause for anger. If I expressed it too—forcefully.' A large hand exactly conveyed the violence of his reaction so that she once more experienced that curious sensation of mingled alarm and excitement he had aroused in her. 'For that I apologise—if that is what you wish me to do.'

'You don't have to!' It wasn't easy to meet his eyes again, but she did so briefly before taking up the coffee pot and refilling her cup with hands that trembled slightly. Then she glanced up and gave him a half-smile that softened the taut line of her mouth and made it look childlike and very vulnerable. 'I'm sorry too, Marco, you must know that.' She spoke in a small and slightly husky voice as she busied her hands with honey and hot rolls. 'I can't think how I could have forgotten I was going to see the Eagle when I'd been so looking forward to it!'

It was clear that he was under no delusion how it happened, and there was an edge of hardness in his voice that matched the sardonic smile he gave her. 'Oh, I do not imagine it was too difficult to forget in the circumstances, Jana; as Francesca has said, when Stefano has it in mind to seduce a woman he seldom fails!'

'Seduce——' Jana stared at him, unsure whether to laugh or grow angry. 'You'd hardly call a couple of rides in a gondola and giving me lunch and dinner seduction!'

'I agree, I would not!'

'Oh, he kissed me once or twice and flirted with me,' Jana hastened to add, following his train of thought all too easily. 'But surely that's standard practice almost in that situation, isn't it? Isn't that what you'd do in the same circumstances, Marco?'

For a moment she actually thought she had him at a loss, but after a moment or two he shrugged, a trace of a smile once more touching his mouth as he shrugged. '*Sì, naturalmente,*' he allowed.

Jana took a long drink from her coffee then looked across at him and half-smiled. 'I hope you're going to give me another chance to see the Eagle,' she ventured. 'I still want to, very much.'

'So?'

The question, so soft-voiced, brought a swift and un-expected urgency to her heartbeat suddenly and she looked at him for a moment a little uncertainly. 'Of course I do, Marco—please.'

Francesca's gaze switched from one to the other, and she was smiling as she picked up her coffee cup and leaned back in her chair, apparently satisfied that she had healed the breach. But Jana would have felt happier if only he had smiled, although it was unthinkable that he would do other than agree.

'Of course you may still see it if you wish to, *piccina*, only this time I shall not remove it from the *camera forte*.' A fleeting smile softened his serious face for a moment. 'This time you will go to the Eagle instead, hah?'

'Of course, I don't mind where I go to see it!' She laughed and her eyes had the blueness of sapphires. 'I'm so excited, I can't wait! Could I see it before we go out, do you think, Marco?'

'I do not see why not.' She noticed the familiar and slightly mocking gleam in his eyes as he helped himself to more coffee. 'But we will go quite soon, before you are once more distracted and the Eagle is forgotten yet again.'

His meaning was unmistakable since he had glanced over his shoulder at the half-open door when he said it, and Francesca made a grimace of reproach at him, even though she must have seen the logic of the manoeuvre. 'You are perhaps right,' she told him. 'Eh, Jana?'

Catching Marco's eye briefly, Jana shook her head. 'Oh, I shan't be sidetracked again,' she promised.

The room that Marco had referred to as the strongroom was situated at the back of the *palazzo*, that is on the side facing away from the canal. It backed on to a narrow *calle* and the rear of another *palazzo*, currently used as an hotel. Tall houses clustered close casting more or less permanent shadow across the *calle*, squat Venetian chimneys cheek by jowl with skeletal television aerials, and there was little lost in the way of a view at this side, only a jumbled incongruous mixture of two worlds forced into uneasy proximity.

It therefore mattered little that the windows of the room were barred and shuttered, but it must have presented a formidable prospect to any would-be thief. Like so many Venetian buildings it had only one modest entrance on the landward side, and that at some distance from the strong-room, so that that too must have presented a further deterrent. Being situated at the end of a long, uncarpeted corridor as it was also gave it an air of isolation from the rest of the *palazzo* too.

Marco turned a huge iron key in the lock, then worked a complicated series of bolts and locks to open the heavy, iron-banded door, and Jana shivered as she walked past him and into the vault, for it smelled musty and cold and somehow menacing. The three hundred years or so since the *palazzo* was built were much more evident here than elsewhere in the building, and she could not help wondering what the original purpose of this grim, isolated room had been.

The click of a switch illuminated it suddenly and dazzlingly, so that she put a hand instinctively to shield her eyes from the glare. 'What was this place originally?' She ventured the question in a slightly hushed voice, as if she feared being overheard, and Marco looked down at her and smiled mockingly.

'You do not have to lower your voice, Jana, there is no one to hear you but the walls, although it was not always so!' Her swift upward glance seemed to cause him some amusement, for he was shaking his head and laughing. 'Those who were—unfriendly towards the Vincella were brought here,' he told her, his hand tightly curled about her arm. 'To them it would have been a place of terror, *piccina!*

You see that it has only the one door, and that very thick and heavily barred, and the windows are also barred and shuttered—no sound would escape from it!'

It was all too easy to imagine the scene, and heaven knew how often it had been repeated, so that Jana shivered and unconsciously drew closer to him until the warm pressure of his arm reassured her. 'You mean it was some kind of a torture chamber?' she asked, and Marco shrugged carelessly.

'Something of the sort, sì.' Briefly his long fingers pressed hard into her soft flesh and made her gasp; then looking down at her reproachful face he laughed softly. 'Oh, do not be afraid, Jana, I have not brought you here with the intention of reviving the practices of my forebears—you are quite safe!'

But Jana was reminded of the fierceness of his passion last night, and the unbridled fury of his kiss, and she suspected that there was far more of the ancient Vincella in the present holder of the title than he would perhaps like to admit. A capacity for violence and the need to dominate that only a different moral climate imposed on him, lurked not too far below that smooth civility, she suspected, and hastily stilled a sudden fluttering urgency in her pulse as she walked beside him.

The room was big enough to give back the suggestion of an echo from the stone walls, even though they were lined with a single row of wooden shelves which she felt sure were a comparatively new innovation. The shelves themselves carried a variety of glass cases, some of them empty, but most containing items of the ancient art of the gold and silversmith, or the craft of the swordsmith in slender swords and daggers in velvet scabbards and with jewelled hilts. It was a dazzling display and took Jana's breath away for a moment.

Right down at the far end of the room and facing her as she walked beside Marco across the stone floor was a big rectangular case, oblong in shape and containing what appeared to be a crudely shaped crucifix worked in gold and jewels. It was only when she came nearer that Jana realised she was looking at last at the Eagle of the Vincella, and the realisation brought a sudden thudding urgency to her heartbeat as she stared at it.

It was set at just about eye-level to her, and she could see as she stood in front of it that it was every bit as rich and opulent as she had been led to expect. Giles had described it as ugly, but she was too dazzled at the moment to decide whether or not it deserved quite such a harsh judgment, certainly it was impressive.

It also had the same air of menace that its stone counterpart possessed, where it loomed above the courtyard, but it had a certain beauty too that she had to recognise. The gold was matt and glowing rather than bright and smooth, and seemed to absorb the intensity of the lights rather than reflect it, but the gems used in its decoration gleamed with a brightness that was almost harsh in its brilliance.

The wings were outspread and the talons extended, which accounted for her first impression of it as a crucifix, and the eyes seemed to stare directly at her with a kind of baleful malevolence. Huge topaz, multi-faceted to give the illusion of life, formed the pupils of the eyes, and closely set rubies and diamonds formed the irises, catching the light and glinting with shifting colour. The talons were set with dozens of small rubies so that they appeared at first sight to be dripping with blood, and Jana shivered yet again when she looked at them.

It was instinctive, when Marco opened the glass case, to take a step backwards, as if she feared the creature might take flight, and he turned and looked at her curiously over his shoulder before lifting the Eagle out of its case, obviously puzzled by her reaction. Sensing his curiosity, she hastily shook her head and half-smiled.

It glittered and gleamed richly as he lifted it out, and obviously from the way he handled it it would seem to be solid, as he claimed, and weigh extremely heavily. Yet somehow, cradled in those long brown hands it seemed slightly less menacing, and Jana moved closer once more, staring down at it in awe, uncertain still whether or not she shared Giles' opinion of it.

'L'Aquila di Vincella,' said Marco and she recognised a certain reverence in his voice that touched a responsive chord in her own senses. 'Are you impressed, Jana?'

It was an almost unconscious gesture when she put out a hand and lightly touched the warm gold breast of the creature with a finger-tip, and she nodded without speaking for a moment. She could not deny she was impressed, but she was also strangely drawn to it in a way she found hard to explain. It was as if she could sense the touch of other hands on that gilded breast, rippling with golden feathers and not nearly as cold and inanimate as she expected.

It had been initially destined as church property if legend was true, so that the illusion of a crucifix that had first struck her was quite understandable, but it had been guardian of the fortunes of the Vincella for more than three centuries and she could not believe that Marco would ever seriously think of parting with it, not even for the sake of his beloved Venice.

Looking down into the glittering topaz eyes, she found it incredibly hard to remember that they were only clusters of jewels, and with one hand she stroked along the sweeping curve of a wing. 'Marco, you——'

She broke off hastily when the sound of footsteps came chattering along the corridor outside the door, and she turned, as Marco did, when Stefano came into the room, standing for a moment to look across at them before he came on. She was quite unaware of the frown that greeted his appearance, and watched as he came down the length of the room, his black hair thick and shining as sable, and smiling when he caught that swift involuntary frown of Marco's.

'Mamma said that I should find you here,' he informed Jana blandly, and gazed at the Eagle with obvious distaste. 'You are looking at the monster, I see. It is *orrendo*, is it not, Jana?' He gave a realistic shudder and curled his lip in defiance of his cousin's opinion. 'If ever it becomes mine I shall sell it and never have to see it again!'

'Oh no!'

Marco had intimated what Stefano's opinion of it was, but she had not altogether believed him, she had to admit. Now as Marco replaced it, relieving his arms of its weight, she was faced with Stefano's look of puzzlement over her reaction. '*Carissima mia*, you surely do not like the thing?' With his own opinion so plain, he had not anticipated a different one from her. 'But you surely do not think it beautiful, Jana—*Benedetta Maria*, I cannot believe it!'

'It isn't ugly and it isn't horrible, Stefano!' She could not have said what made her so earnest in the Eagle's defence, but as she looked at it in its case once more, the glass door was open still and the light warmed the dull glow of gold, and it drew her like a magnet. Reaching up, she lightly touched it once more. 'Oh, I can't explain, but it's surely something special to the Vincella! Surely none of you could even think of selling it!'

She wasn't looking at Stefano when she said that, but directly at Marco, and there was a deep and fathomless darkness in his eyes that defied interpretation, so that she shook her head slowly, as much at a loss as ever to know whether or not he had decided the Eagle's fate. Stefano, it was clear, was still trying to understand her feelings, but Marco was in little doubt. He glanced once more at the Eagle in its case, then looked at Jana with a steadiness she found infinitely disturbing.

'Jana fears for the future of the Eagle, Stefano. She finds it hard to visualise a situation where we could part with it, is that not right, *piccina*?'

It was the gentle enquiring tone of his voice that prompted her to speak as frankly as she did, and she still addressed him rather than Stefano. 'I just can't imagine how anyone can—throw away three hundred years of their family history, no matter what the cause. And isn't it said to be the guardian of the family's fortunes? You can't sell it, Marco, you just *can't*!'

'Jana!' Stefano rested an arm about her shoulders in easy familiarity, and looked at her curiously, sensing how serious she was and seeing no reason for it. 'There is no question of Marco selling it, *carissima*.' He looked at his cousin and laughed shortly. 'Marco would as soon be parted from his right arm as from *L'Aquila di Vincella, carissima mia*! You should know that of him by now!'

His eyes sparkled maliciously and Jana was on the very brink of betraying just how close Marco was to parting with the Eagle, when she caught his eye and hastily shook her head, looking down at her hands rather than at him. But he said nothing until he had locked the glass case once more and pocketed the key, then he turned around to face her.

'Now that you have seen the Eagle, Jana, I think that it is time we began work. I have a long list of visits planned for this morning, so it will be as well if we do not leave it too late before we begin, hah?'

'Yes, of course!' She readily agreed, unaware of Stefano's sudden frown of dislike, and more than thankful that things seemed to have returned to normal. After last night she had been afraid they would never be the same again. 'I have to fetch my bag, that's all, and I'll be with you—it won't take a minute.'

'Jana!' She turned quickly and saw the deep frown between Stefano's black brows and the glitter of dislike in his eyes as he looked down at her. 'Yesterday you made a promise that you would be with me today also, do you not remember?'

Quite truthfully, Jana could not remember if she had made such a promise or not. Yesterday had something of dreamlike quality, even in retrospect, and she had allowed herself to be swept along without really taking much note of anything except the fact that she was thoroughly enjoying herself. Perhaps she had made such a promise, but if she had she did not remember it.

Still trying to recall what she had actually said, she found quite suddenly that the decision of what to say or do had been taken from her, firmly and without hesitation, by Marco. 'Jana cannot be spared for a second day, Stefano. I need her to assist me; you must look elsewhere for your amusement!'

It was a harsh rejection, and for a moment Jana almost cried out in protest, but a glance at Stefano was enough to tell her that he had little need of her sympathy. 'Jana?' He stubbornly ignored the decision, looking still at Jana and seeking her opinion.

'I'm sorry, Stefano.'

There seemed nothing else she could say. Glancing up at the implacable face of his cousin, she wondered vaguely why it mattered so much that Marco had so firmly staked his claim. He had no real right to behave in that autocratic fashion where she was concerned, and yet she could do nothing about the curious satisfaction it gave her to hear him do so; and she glanced up instinctively when his long hard fingers brushed briefly against her hand as he walked beside her. Possibly it was by accident, but she thought not.

'Another day, Stefano, I'd be pleased to come,' she told him in a not quite steady voice. 'Not today.'

'Ah, *dannazione*!'

The oath hissed back from the stone walls like the ghost of an echo, and Stefano went striding on alone, leaving them to follow at a more leisurely pace. His body was taut with anger and there was an air of arrogant defiance in the angle of his head that left his feelings in no doubt at all. Seconds later a door slammed somewhere and Marco looked up briefly from locking the strongroom door, then glanced at Jana and raised a brow. She thought for a moment that he might, after all, be going to give her the choice of going with Stefano, but she knew she was wrong as soon as he spoke.

'Hurry and fetch your bag, *piccina*, and we will go! We have much to make up for yesterday, hah?'

A small café in the older and quieter part of Venice offered a brief respite from the more crowded and popular places, and Jana leaned her elbows on the table and supported her chin with one hand wh'le she gazed across the sunlit square at the elegant lines of a small *palazzo* opposite, quite prepared to linger just as long as Marco allowed her to. It was one of the most satisfying things about being with Marco, the fact that he was prepared to sit quietly occasionally when she herself was inclined to do so. It was in such contrast to Stefano's constant need to be doing something, and she found it much more relaxing.

She took advantage of his preoccupation after a moment to study him surreptitiously, and yet again wondered at the response of her senses to that air of virile forcefulness that seemed to surround him, even when he was at ease. Inevitably she was once more reminded of his reception of her last night. That savagely dominating side of his character was something she found too disturbing to dwell on, and she wished it did not keep recurring every so often to remind her.

She scanned that dark aristocratic face trying to make up her mind how it was he could make so much more of an impression on her than his cousin did, and without even trying. A lightweight beige suit worn with a cream shirt, open at the neck, gave his olive-dark complexion a look of swarthiness, and his dark eyes were hidden by lazily lowered lids as he looked across the square, but by turning his head suddenly he caught her unaware, and a fleeting glimpse of smile brought her study of him to a hasty conclusion.

Seeking a safer subject for her interest, she indicated the little *palazzo* opposite. 'What's that place? It's rather pretty.' Catching his grimace of dislike for her choice of adjective, she tilted her chin. 'I think it's pretty,' she insisted. 'It's Renaissance, isn't it? I wondered if it was on our agenda.'

He wasn't drinking coffee this morning, but had another popular Venetian drink, a glass of ice-water flavoured with aniseed, and he emptied the glass before he answered her, a faintly mocking gleam in his eyes when he smiled across at her. 'That is the Palazzo Favoratini,' he informed her, and put down his glass, watching her as he traced a line down the side of the glass in the mist of condensation. 'It is partly Renaissance, although most of it has been—how is it?—made over in the style of baroque. I have no doubt that it would appeal to you, *piccina*, because of its romantic history, and you are a *romantica*, hah?' He leaned towards her with his elbows on the table and it brought that sternly handsome face much too close for comfort. 'Am I not right, Jana?'

Determinedly matter-of-fact, Jana looked across at the

palazzo and did her best to keep her voice steady. 'I really don't know,' she said. 'Have we got time to go and look at it?'

'We will make time, if you wish to go and see it.'

He was not usually so amenable where their schedule was concerned and she looked at him a little uncertainly. She thought she detected a glimpse of mockery in the way he smiled, and wondered what he found so amusing in this instance. 'Is it very special?' she asked, and he spread his hands wide rather than confirm it.

'You will find it *romantissimo* because it was once the home of a very beautiful woman; the mistress of one of the most powerful and influential men in Venice in the early part of the eighteenth century. The lady's name was Margherita Favoratini and she was rumoured to be descended from the famous—or infamous, depending upon your view —Cesare Borgia.'

'Really?' Making no secret of her interest, Jana leaned forward until she was looking directly at him from only a matter of inches away, and she spared only a brief glance for the slender columns and gilded portico of the little *palazzo* opposite, turning back swiftly when Marco laughed. 'What are you laughing at?'

'You, *ragazza*, and your interest in ancient gossip!' His laughter teased her as she looked at him reproachfully, but he enlightened her further without any prompting. 'It is only rumour that she was descended from the Borgia, Jana. The liaison between the lady's ancestor and the duke was——' One hand conveyed his meaning unmistakably. 'But certainly the lovely Margherita had the Borgia good looks and also their colouring.'

'You mean there's a picture of her?'

'A very lovely one, that suggests that the artist also may have been a victim of the lady's charm.' He was smiling; that faintly sardonic glint showing once more in his eyes as he regarded her steadily. 'Do you wish to see her, Jana?'

'I'd love to!' She picked up her coffee and hastily swallowed the last of it, then reached round for the satchel-bag hanging on the back of her chair. 'It won't hinder us too much, will it?'

'Not too much,' Marco agreed affably, and got to his feet. Taking her hand, he pulled her to her feet, then slid his fingers beneath her arm as they walked across the square. 'I should have known that you would find a *storia d'amore* too much to resist!'

Slightly on the defensive without quite knowing why, Jana looked at him through her lashes. 'No more than most women would have been in the circumstances,' she said. 'Though, again like most women, I like a happy ending. Did Margherita Favoratini's story have a happy ending?'

The shadow of the little *palazzo* enveloped them as they neared the doorway, and Jana looked up into his face enquiringly. Marco shrugged, perhaps carelessly, she couldn't be quite sure. 'Who can tell, *piccina*? She lived to be sixty years old, which was quite a good age for that time, and if we are to believe legend, she never lost the affection of her lover, so it may be assumed that she was happy, I think.'

A modest charge admitted them to the *palazzo* and gave them the freedom of its rooms which they seemingly had to themselves, since there appeared to be no one else about. It was different in several ways—for one thing, the main entrance was from the little *campo* and not from the water, and although it was small it lacked nothing in luxury and grandeur. Baroque ostentation had overtaken the original Renaissance classicism, and there was plenty of evidence that either Margherita Favoratini's taste or that of her lover had run to the flamboyant.

Marble and gilt had been used in plenty and the rooms now had the look of a museum rather than a home, but Jana could easily imagine it alive with the presence of a beautiful woman, for there were many of her things still in evidence. Her embroidery frame and silk box stood side by side with a brocaded chair and footstool, and a small gilded chair with a red brocaded seat shared a place before the *sala* fireplace with a larger, matching one. Even her small and incredibly ornate *pianoforte* had been preserved and must now be worth a fortune, for it was surely one of the earliest ones made—her lover had obviously indulged her every whim.

Jana found it all fascinating, but she was most anxious to see the lady herself, and she said as much to Marco. 'Then let us find her, *piccina*,' he said, and led her straight to a room that was long and narrow and filled with paintings, mostly portraits.

'You know your way around here,' Jana remarked, and he merely smiled.

With one hand he held her arm and with the other indicated a large gilt frame containing a portrait that was much larger than any of the others in the vicinity, as if to draw attention to it as something special, and he watched for her reaction with an intensity she found vaguely disturbing. 'Madonna Margherita Favoratini!' he said, as if he was introducing her.

Perhaps it was simply because Marco had mentioned the fact of her living until she was sixty years old, but for some reason the youth of the girl in the picture came as a surprise, for she looked little more than fifteen or sixteen years old. Neither did she have the boldness that Jana anticipated, in fact she looked very shy and gentle, and not at all the sort of descendant one would expect of the arrogant Duke of Valentinois, Cesare Borgia.

Her hair was a deep gold, not unlike her own, and her eyes were blue, demurely half-hidden by lowered lids and light brown lashes. She wore a dress of olive green brocade, cut low over the bosom in the fashion of the day, and with half sleeves, and on her head was a small cap that looked to be made of lace.

Marco obviously found her quite fascinating, and Jana smiled, a smile meant to mock his obvious infatuation with the lady. 'Is she the girl of your dreams, Marco? Your ideal woman—you obviously find her fascinating!'

His gaze left the portrait and settled instead on her own face, and after a moment he smiled slowly, his eyes dark and fathomless. 'She is the kind of woman I could marry, *cara mia*,' he said, soft-voiced, and Jana swallowed hastily, disconcerted by his seriousness.

Looking up at the portrait once more, she studied the smooth young face critically and tried to see something of the *coquette* there; some suggestion of sensuality that would have made her more acceptable in Jana's eyes as the mistress of a powerful and influential man. Instead she saw only a rather shy-looking girl who, on appearance alone, looked as if she would know little of such things.

'She doesn't *look* like a mistress,' she observed after a moment or two, and blinked in surprise when Marco laughed.

'Oh, *piccina*, how do you judge? Madonna Margherita was in love and beloved, but does that necessarily make her a——' He shrugged, an expressive Latin gesture that left nothing in doubt. 'I think you do her an injustice, *cara mia*.'

Heaven knew why she felt so defensive, but Jana glanced again at Margherita Favoratini and her mouth showed a hint of reproach when she looked up at Marco once more. 'Then why didn't he marry her?' she asked.

'Because, *cara*, the gentleman was already married when he saw her first. He was almost fifteen years older than she was, but he loved her from the moment he saw her, although he was already thirty years old and she barely sixteen, very much as she is here, I imagine. So it is said,' he added when she frowned at him curiously, and Jana followed up her curiosity determinedly.

'You seem to know quite a lot about *him* too, whoever he was,' she said, and looked both ways along the narrow gallery at the assembled portraits, moving off further along the room as if to search for him. 'Is he here too, Marco?'

She took no more than a couple of steps, then Marco caught her arm and turned her about in the direction of the door. His hold on her was firm, despite her slightly lagging step. 'He is not here, *piccina*, and I think that it is time we continued with our work if we are to have something to present to Giles this evening.'

'But I'd like to——'

'There is no more time, *piccola*! I brought you here because I thought you would be interested in Margherita Favoratini and her story, but we have spent too much time here already.'

Admitting he was right did not come easily, but she allowed him to lead her once more to the entrance without resistance, and they went from the close, stuffy air of the little *palazzo* once more into the shadows of the *campo* and the comparative cool. But curiosity still made her reluctant, even though she yielded to his insistence, and she looked up at him as they walked once more out into the square.

'I won't believe there isn't a portrait of Margherita Favoratini's lover somewhere,' she said. 'If he was as powerful and important as you say he was, Marco, he must surely have had his portrait painted at some time. Who was he? Where can I see his portrait?'

The sigh he gave was deep and deliberately exaggerated, and he held her arm in a firm grip that pressed his long, strong fingers into her flesh as they crossed the square together. 'His portrait hangs in the Palazzo Vincella, *Sig-*

norina Curiosa! He was Gaspare Valentino Fabriano, the
fourth Conte di Vincella. He was also known as the Eagle
of the Vincella because of his immense power and his
reputation of ruthlessness with all those who opposed him!'
As if to emphasise his words his fingers gripped her arm
more firmly and when she looked up at him to protest she
met with a vaguely menacing smile that gleamed like jet in
his eyes. 'And now we will continue with our work, hah?'

Slightly dazed, but wondering if she should really have
been surprised, Jana nodded. 'If you say so,' she agreed,
and Marco laughed. It wouldn't really have done any good
to say otherwise, she thought.

CHAPTER EIGHT

IT was difficult containing her curiosity about the fourth Conte di Vincella for the rest of the day, but somehow Jana managed to. It seemed to her that Marco had enlightened her as much as he intended to at the moment and she was reluctant to appear too curious. In fact the story of Margherita Favoratini's romance with his predecessor intrigued her and she meant to find out more, but not necessarily from Marco, other members of the family were sure to be as well informed, and she thought particularly of Francesca Abrizzi.

It was the very unlikelihood of the affair that fascinated her. The idea of a man who had earned himself such a reputation for ruthlessness falling in love, and staying in love, with a young girl almost young enough to be his daughter must surely be unusual, and especially such a girl as Margherita Favoratini appeared to be from her picture.

But whatever Jana's intention had been, the matter was put completely out of her mind when she met Francesca on the gallery just before dinner. They had left their rooms at almost the same moment and Jana turned and waited for the older woman to join her, admiring the dress she wore with undisguised frankness.

It was a deep yellow and it gave a smooth golden sheen to Francesca's olive-dark skin that was infinitely flattering and gave lie to the forty-one years she laid claim to. But it was not only the dress that made her look as she did, Jana realised as she joined her, there was a bright sparkling look about her, conspicuous enough to make Jana curious.

'I love that dress, Francesca,' she told her as they walked

151

along the gallery together. 'I envy you being able to look so gorgeous in yellow; it's my favourite colour, but it doesn't suit me a bit.'

Francesca looked pleased, preening herself at the compliment and tossing back her short black hair as she laughed. 'I look a little—*speciale*, eh? I hope that I do, *cara*, for this is to be a very special evening for me and for——' She hesitated, catching her lower lip between even white teeth, then she quite unexpectedly turned to Jana and hugged her, letting her go with a breathless laugh when she saw her blink of surprise. 'Oh, *Santa Madre*, I have to tell someone, and I would like it to be you, *cara* Jana! I am sure that Giles will forgive me!'

'Giles?' Jana was smiling too without quite knowing why, except that excitement like Francesca's was infectious, and she had a growing suspicion that she knew the reason for it. 'What are you so excited about, Francesca?'

Francesca still hesitated as she stood facing her on the gallery, her bright dark eyes showing a hint of anxiety, but yet not enough to dim the bubbling excitement that made the hand on Jana's arm tremble slightly. Then she took a deep breath and her words were a little more heavily accented than usual.

'You know that I have been helping Giles a little with his writing these past weeks——'

'You've helped a great deal, from what Giles has told me,' Jana interrupted with a smile. 'He's enjoyed having your help too.'

Francesca shook her head, though obviously she was delighted to hear it. 'Not so much help,' she denied, 'but it is enjoyable out on the *terrazzo*, and it is good that Giles rests and takes the sun.' As if she detected a hint of impatience in her listener, she hurried on. 'I still do not know if I have imagined it, Jana, but just before we completed our work, less than an hour ago—Giles asked me to marry him!'

'Oh, Francesca!'

Jana hadn't seen Giles since she and Marco returned, for they had been late back and he had already gone to his room to freshen up before dinner when they arrived. Not that it was really unexpected, she told herself, although obviously the developing friendship she had noticed between Francesca and her uncle had progressed much further and much more quickly than she realised. Too stunned for the moment to do more than stare at her, Jana did not immediately realise that her reaction was open to misinterpretation until she saw Francesca's expression of vague disappointment.

'I thought that you had some idea, Jana—are you not pleased?' she asked. 'Do you not like the idea of your uncle being married to me—of my becoming your aunt?'

Realising at last what a wrong impression she was giving, Jana hugged her impulsively and laughed. 'Oh, Francesca, I'm thrilled, of course I like it—I think it's wonderful! Oh, you don't know how often I've wished Giles had someone—someone like you, Francesca! He's such a kind and wonderful man, but he's always been so—so reserved, so used to hiding in his shell. I'm absolutely thrilled that you've managed to persuade him out of it, I really am!'

'*Grazie, cara, tante grazie!*' Arm in arm they continued along the gallery, heads close together and both of them sparkling with the excitement of the occasion. 'Tonight at dinner Giles will tell everyone, but—Oh, I just could not wait!' Francesca glanced at Jana from the corner of her eye and pulled a face. 'I am behaving like a foolish young girl, no?'

'No!' Jana affirmed stoutly. 'You have every right to be happy, Francesca, and so has Giles, and I know you'll be *very* happy. But it means a lot of planning, doesn't it? When and where are you getting married, Francesca?'

'Oh, *cara*, I have not thought so far yet!' She laughed and shook her head, obviously still a little dazed by the suddenness of it. 'But it will be very quiet, *naturalmente*; not only for Giles' sake, but because it will be more fitting for a woman of forty-one years, eh?'

'Nonsense, you don't look any older than I do!' Jana assured her. 'No one would believe you're old enough to be Stefano's mother.'

Francesca sighed reminiscently. 'I was nineteen years when I had Stefano,' she remembered, and Jana wondered for a moment whether her first advantageous marriage had been her own choice or whether she had been persuaded into it by her family. 'He is twenty-two—that is your own age, is it not, Jana? Think, *cara*, I could also be your mother, and here I am anticipating my wedding like a young girl!'

'You'll make a lovely bride, Francesca, and I know you'll make Giles a very happy man.'

Francesca smiled her thanks, but her eyes had a more speculative look as she scanned Jana's face from the corner of her eye for a moment. 'And you, *cara mia*—when will you make someone a happy man?'

It wasn't a subject Jana cared to even consider at the moment, and she shrugged carelessly, only vaguely aware of the slight flush that coloured her cheeks, and the sudden need to hide her eyes below their thick lashes. 'One wedding at a time is enough,' she told her. 'I've plenty of time to think about my own when yours and Giles' is safely over!'

'There is no one——'

'No one!' Jana insisted hastily, and laughed. 'I shall take my time, Francesca!'

'But you will arrive, hah?' Francesca smiled knowingly

and looked across at the door of the *sala* as they approached it.

Men's voices were already clearly audible and easily distinguishable from each other. Giles' light, quiet and very English voice; Stefano's excitable and very Italian one, and Marco's; deep, soft and curiously affecting even at a distance so that she felt a flutter of response from her senses. She could never mistake that voice for anyone else's, Jana felt, and wondered what Marco would have to say about the forthcoming announcement.

'We are the last to arrive, I think,' Francesca whispered as they neared the door, then laughed and caught at Jana's arm. 'I am *nervosa, cara*, is that not foolish of me?'

Thinking she knew how she felt, Jana nodded, and it occurred to her suddenly to wonder what Stefano was going to say about it if he did not already know. 'Have you told Stefano about you and Giles yet?' she asked, and Francesca shook her head.

'Not yet, there had not been time; it was—how is it?—sprung on me!'

'You think he's going to mind?'

It wasn't impossible, Jana thought, that Stefano would take an unfavourable view of his mother's remarriage. His own father had been wealthy and volatile as well as an excellent business man, and Giles was just about everything that Emilio Abrizzi had not been. He liked Giles well enough, as far as she could tell, but that was not quite the same as seeing him as his stepfather, and she hoped for both Giles' and Francesca's sakes that he would accept it without objection.

Francesca swung back her dark hair in a gesture that suggested defiance and was completely at odds with her usual manner. 'How should Stefano mind?' she asked. 'Almost certainly he will marry himself before very long, and then what would he expect me to do? I shall marry

Giles, *mia cara* Jana, whatever Stefano thinks of the idea, because I love him very much! But I do not think that Stefano will dislike it so much.' She added the last as if it was merely a fervent hope.

When they walked into the *sala* all three men turned swiftly, and Jana noticed how in this instance Giles' first look was for Francesca—a warm, eager but slightly anxious look that Jana saw as typical of him. He met Jana's eye only briefly, then saw Francesca seated at the table. Jana, on the other hand, had the immediate attention of both Marco and Stefano, the one giving her a long appreciative gaze that stirred her pulses urgently, and the other a much more obvious gesture with hunched finger-tips to his pursed lips and a dazzlingly broad smile.

The soft pale-green dress she wore flattered her colouring and the slight flush in her cheeks she attributed to Francesca's unexpected news. Marco noticed it and raised a brow as he moved with deceptive speed to see her seated, a task that Stefano had intended for himself, and he frowned blackly when he was out-manoeuvred.

The chair pressed lightly against the back of her legs and Jana sat down, made aware of another fluttering increase in her pulse when Marco's long brown hands brushed her shoulders. He bent his head, his face close to hers, and whispered something before he moved away, but it was in Italian and she was too slow to catch the words. Looking up, she frowned at him curiously, but he was already on his way to his own seat at the head of the table, and she followed him with her eyes until he sat down.

Stefano took his place beside her, still frowning, that unexpected whisper of Marco's undoubtedly adding to his displeasure. He flirted with her determinedly all through dinner, although she was vaguely conscious of a noticeable edge on his usually persuasive voice, and he cast frequent glances in his cousin's direction whenever he kissed her fingers or leaned forward to murmur some endearment in her ear in a whisper that was surely meant to be heard at the far end of the table.

Jana supposed she was less responsive than usual, but her thoughts this evening were with Giles and how he must be feeling at the prospect of making an announcement in public. Catching his eye again briefly, she smiled, but from the way he looked it seemed likely that Francesca had confessed to telling her the news in advance, and his vaguely sheepish look made her smile to herself.

Preoccupied as she was, however, Stefano was not easily ignored altogether, and he resolutely drew her wandering attention to him once more with a complaint murmured in her ear but none the less forceful and determined to be heard. 'I have not seen you all day, Jana!'

Turning to smile at him briefly, she shrugged. 'Well, of course you haven't, Stefano. You never do when I'm working, and we've been *very* busy today.'

'So you led me to believe this morning, when you refused to keep the promise you made to me yesterday!'

'Then you'll know it was true!' she said a little impatiently. She simply wasn't in the mood to deal with Stefano's complaints this evening, not when there was so much to be excited about.

'If that is so then I cannot imagine why you were visiting the Palazzo Favoratini this morning!' he said shortly, and for a moment Jana turned and gave him her full attention. Her vaguely startled blink seemed to afford him some amusement, for he was smiling maliciously. 'I saw you, *carissima*, when you were leaving the *palazzo*. You were crossing the square with Marco and you were both looking very pleased with yourselves, smiling and so—friendly.'

Jana's impatience was growing by the minute and she had a curious dislike of the idea of him seeing her with Marco like that, when she was unaware of it and perhaps less on her guard than she more usually was. 'I can't think why you sound so surprised at the fact of us being friendly, Stefano,' she told him with a hint of a frown. 'We couldn't work together as well as we do if we *weren't* friendly!'

'And that was why he held so tightly to your arm, eh?'

She remembered how determinedly Marco had removed her from the little *palazzo* before she became any more involved in the affair of Margherita Favoratini, and she could not resist a smile. 'He was making sure I didn't go back and spend more time looking at things that have nothing to do with the job in hand!' she told him wryly. 'Marco, in case you aren't aware of it, is a great stickler for keeping to the schedule, and the Palazzo Favoratini wasn't on the schedule!'

'So?'

The implication was too obvious to be ignored and she shrugged carelessly. 'I don't know why I'm bothering to explain,' she told him, 'but since you seem determined to make an interrogation of this conversation, we'd been to see Madonna Margherita Favoratini; do you know her?' The glance she gave in Marco's direction was more instinctive than deliberate and unconsciously provocative, for she could not help but remember his fascination with the girl in the painting. 'Marco adores her! I think that's the main reason he took me to see her, so that he could get another glimpse of his lovely Borgia lady!'

Stefano clucked impatiently with his tongue and refused to be pacified; it was clear that the matter had been on his mind all day and he resented what he saw as a slight to himself. 'So—Marco tells me that you are much too busy to keep your promise to me, but he takes you to visit a place that has nothing to do with your work! Hah!'

Jana sighed resignedly, but did not take any of it too seriously, for Stefano's bad moods were seldom long-lived and she supposed he did have cause for complaint if she had indeed promised to spend the day with him again. Not that she was giving him her whole attention even now, for she was waiting for Giles to make his announcement, and she spoke with only half her mind on what she was saying.

'We had coffee at the little café opposite the *palazzo*,' she explained, watching her uncle and Francesca talking together, and guessing how Giles must be feeling, even with Francesca to encourage him. 'Marco said Madonna Margherita was descended from Cesare Borgia, and I'm fascinated by anything to do with the Borgias, so—he took me to see her!'

'*Naturalmente!*' He still sounded surly, but Jana was determined he wasn't going to spoil her pleasure.

'Oh, please don't make so much fuss, Stefano,' she begged. 'I'm not in the mood to argue with you tonight— I'm too happy!'

Her gaze was on her uncle, seated next to Marco at the head of the table, but possibly to Stefano it appeared that she was looking at his cousin with those happy, sapphire bright eyes, and he frowned his dislike. 'So,' he said, in a half-whisper, 'he has made you happy, has he?'

'Hmm?'

She was distracted, for her uncle was leaning across the table saying something to Marco, and knowing how nervous he would be at having to do anything as out of the ordinary as make an announcement of his engagement, Jana crossed her fingers under cover of the table cloth, giving him her whole attention. Stefano, as yet unaware of anything but his own emotions, leaned closer and whispered in her ear.

'I could make you so much happier, *carissima,* if you will let me, I promise you! I could make you the most happy woman in the world—will you not let me prove it to you, Jana. Forget Marco—let me love you!'

Jana was conscious only of his voice and assumed that he was still complaining about her visiting the Palazzo Favoratini with Marco, she did not register the actual words he spoke, nor see the look in his eyes. Half turning her head, but keeping her eye on her uncle, she smiled absently. 'Forget about it, Stefano, please, it isn't that important!'

'*Dannazione!*' She heard his muttered curse and put a casual hand over his when she remembered the surprise he was going to get when her uncle began to speak. But he snatched at her hand and held on to it tightly, squeezing her fingers strongly until she almost cried out and tried to free herself. 'Jana!'

'Please, Stefano!'

Her voice trailed off when her uncle got up and cleared his throat, and she noticed how the hand that held his wine glass trembled so that the dark red liquid shivered and caught the light with the glow of rubies. Seeing it, Francesca reached over and lightly touched his arm with her finger-tips and he looked at her briefly before he began, as if only she gave him the nerve to say what he had to say.

'My friends——' He cleared his throat once more and coloured slightly. 'My friends I am delighted to tell you that Signora Abrizzi—Francesca—has consented to become my wife!'

From the seat beside her Jana heard a curious sound almost like a hiss, and realised it was Stefano's hastily indrawn breath. She half turned to look at him and prayed fervently that he wasn't going to say or do anything to spoil it for Giles and Francesca. The announcement, however short, had cost Giles a lot in effort and obviously Francesca realised just how much, for she leaned towards him and kissed his cheek lightly, smiling into his eyes. The sight of them gave Jana a curious lump in her throat, and she looked up almost involuntarily at Marco: catching his eye and registering a glimmer of speculation; her lack of surprise alone would be enough to tell him she had had prior knowledge, she realised.

Then he was on his feet and raising his glass high, smiling at them both with obvious approval. 'Francesca and Giles,' he said. '*Alla salute!*'

Getting to her feet, Jana too raised her glass, echoing his toast of good health, and only Stefano did not at first realise what was happening. He sat beside Jana staring first at his cousin and then at his mother, and lastly at Jana because she was nearest, then he too got slowly to his feet, his eyes still slightly narrowed and blank, and he raised his glass and drank without making the toast.

Francesca looked across at him, the brightness in her eyes dimmed for a moment as she sought his reaction. 'Stefano, *figlio mio*, will you not also wish us good health—Giles and me?'

'A romance that everyone knew of but me, hah, Mamma?'

Francesca looked slightly hurt, but that determined gleam was still in her eyes that Jana had seen just before they came into the room and she shook her head at him. 'It was there for you to see, *figlio mio*, as Jana and Marco have seen it,' she told him gently. 'You were perhaps too occupied with looking elsewhere, eh, *carissimo*?'

Her dark eyes rested briefly on Jana and she smiled, but there was a bright glittering look in Stefano's eyes as he raised his glass once more. '*Alla salute*, Mamma and Giles!' He downed his drink in one swift draught, then reached down with one hand to pull Jana to her feet once more, holding her close to his side and smiling down into her face.

'Now will you also drink to Jana and me?'

Jana turned to him swiftly, but not before she had seen the quick frown on Marco's face as he reached and refilled the glass in his hand. 'Stefano!' She did not know what to say to him and he took her uncertainty for consent, obviously, for he pulled her round into his arms and kissed her hard, and she was too dazed for a moment to object.

'Stefano, *caro*,' Francesca ventured uncertainly, snatched from her moment of happiness into a situation she did not begin to understand, and puzzled by her son's behaviour. 'What are you saying, *carissimo*? That you and Jana are——'

'I am saying Mama, that while Marco has been leading Jana around Venice like a little schoolgirl, I have found other ways to improve her education, eh, *carissima*?' He laughed and kissed her mouth once more before she could move aside; her legs felt as if they were almost incapable of holding her for much longer and she hadn't a sensible thought in her head as she stood there in the tight curve of his arm too confused to object.

'Stefano——'

'Jana is an admirer of Madonna Margherita, Mamma, did you know?' He interrupted his mother once more, and Jana realised for the first time that he had drunk far more than he usually did during a meal. Laughing loudly, he pulled Jana to him once more and kissed her. 'I have hopes that she will follow the Madonna's example and take a Vincella for a lover, eh, *carissima mia*?' Again his mouth smothered the attempt she made to protest and he raised his glass in a toast. 'Stefano and Jana— *alla salute*!'

The sudden crack of breaking glass brought absolute silence to the big room, and for a breathless second no one even moved; then Jana brought her eyes to the top of the table where a fine Venetian glass lay with its stem broken, red wine spilling like blood over the white cloth around Marco's plate, and she lifted her eyes after a second to look at his face.

His eyes burned like coals and his mouth had a cruel hard straightness she had seen there only once before, when Stefano had brought her home late from their day out. Giles and Francesca were looking at him dazedly, their own

happiness briefly forgotten in the sight of the black fury in
his face, and only Stefano still wore that look of defiance as
he gazed at his cousin and recognised the extent of his
anger.

'Are you bereft of sense as well as good manners?' Marco
demanded, and only the slightest tremor in that deep quiet
voice betrayed the passion that still burned in his eyes.
'Perhaps you will be good enough to explain why you
choose to stage such a display of bad manners at a moment
like this! *Vieni*, let us hear your reason, *per favore*!'

Francesca said nothing, but sat with Giles' hand holding
hers, content to leave it all to her cousin. She knew, none
better, that her son was spoiled, over-indulged since he was
a child, but she had not anticipated such a violent reaction
to her engagement and she made no pretence of understanding him at the moment.

Hardly daring to shrug that possessive arm from her
shoulders, Jana eased away from him, trembling and uncertain, much more affected by Marco's anger than she
cared to admit, but Stefano pulled her back, determined, it
seemed, to hold what he had. 'The reason concerns only
Jana and me,' Stefano declared, sulkily defiant, and Marco
made a short, derisive sound with his mouth that brought a
swift flush of colour to his face.

'You have involved Jana in an embarrassing situation
whether or not she wished to be involved, and you have
brought the manners of a barbarian to my table, *cugino*; I
am concerned!'

Stefano's eyes narrowed and Jana felt his body stiffen,
the fingers on her arm tighten their grip as if he summoned
all his nerve. 'And you are *geloso*, *cugino*, hah?'

'Stefano, *basta*, *per favore*!' Francesca stared at him in
disbelief, while Giles looked across at Jana as if he only
now realised she was the cause of dissension between his
host and his future step-son. 'How could you behave so?'

Francesca demanded, her dark eyes glowing. 'How could you accuse Marco——'

'Francesca, *per favore*!' Marco reached out and took her hand, a brief tight smile seeking to reassure her. 'This is not the time for you and Stefano to quarrel, nor is it the time for us to air our differences, not here at the table and on such a happy occasion. I—reacted too violently, and for this I apologise, *cara mia*, to you and to my old friend—I am sorry!'

His self-control was incredible, Jana thought dazedly, and it made his sudden eruptive display of temper all the more puzzling, for he so seldom lost control. She did not for a moment believe that it had anything to do with jealousy, as Stefano suggested, but whatever it was the violence of it still lingered in the burning intensity of his eyes, even though his voice was as cool and quiet as ever.

With Stefano briefly distracted, Jana sat down, tossing off that encircling arm and taking a hasty sip from her wine glass to help restore her wavering confidence. It was a second or two before Stefano dropped down on to the chair beside her, and she heard Francesca's sigh of relief as plainly as her son must have done. Humility never came easily to him, nor to any of the Vincella, she guessed, but after a moment or two he looked across the table at his mother and inclined his head in a curiously touching little bow.

'*Mi dispiace*, Mamma—Giles.' He raised his empty glass and smiled at them regretfully. '*Alla salute!*' he said, and Jana realised a little ruefully, that he had charmed his way out of yet another situation, even though he had excluded Marco and herself from his apologies.

Jana found Francesca breakfasting alone the following morning and was rather glad. She had the idea that the sooner she put Francesca right about herself and Stefano the better, and she sighed inwardly with relief when Francesca herself raised the question almost as soon as they had exchanged greetings.

Handing her the honey jar, she looked first at Jana's face from the cover of her lashes, then smiled. 'I have to ask, Jana, and I know you will understand my reason, *cara*; you and Stefano——'

'There's nothing between me and Stefano, Francesca, I promise you.' She was so confident that Francesca could not do other than believe her and she nodded, obviously satisfied.

'Ah, *bene*!'

Jana smiled across at her as she spread honey on a hot bread roll and being quite unnecessarily meticulous about it. 'There's certainly nothing like Stefano suggested last night, Francesca, he was simply——' she glanced at the face opposite with a slightly rueful smile. 'I think he was just a little bit tight,' she suggested. 'He'd been brooding all day about the fact that I didn't go with him when he said I promised to,'

'And had you, *cara*?'

'No—that is, I don't remember saying I would.' Jana shrugged as she bit into her roll. 'Anyway, Marco wouldn't stand for me being lazy two days running and he put his foot down. Stefano had been angry about it all day, and then seeing us leaving the *palazzo*——' Once more she shrugged off any more specific explanation and laughed. 'I think he said what he did to get back at me—and Marco, but there wasn't anything in it.'

'That was what I wished to know, *cara*,' Francesca said. 'If it had been anything more—*permanente*, such as Giles and I have, then I would not have been so concerned, I would have been delighted; but I do not have to tell you so, eh?'

Knowing how devoted she was to her only son, Jana took

it as a compliment that she was looked on favourably as a daughter-in-law, but she hastened to make the situation clear before any misunderstandings arose on that score too. 'I'm flattered you feel that way, Francesca, but there isn't anything at all, permanent or otherwise.'

'I see.' She sounded disappointed but not altogether surprised, Jana felt, and almost wished there was such a situation, for she could think of no one she would rather have as a mother-in-law than Francesca Abrizzi. 'Then I cannot count upon a double wedding, that is a pity. However——' She shrugged with Latin resignation and got on with her breakfast for a moment or two, then looked across again and smiled curiously. 'So you have been to see the Palazzo Favoratini?' she said.

'I persuaded Marco to take me to see Madonna Margherita,' Jana said, and laughed because she wasn't really sure whose idea it had been originally. 'At least, I think I persuaded him, but it's possible he wanted to go anyway. I was interested to see what she looked like after learning that she was a descendant of Cesare Borgia—or reputed to be.'

Francesca bit into her roll and looked across at her with bright, curious eyes. 'And did you also see the likeness?' she asked.

She hadn't noticed any likeness at all to Francesca, if that was what she was asking, and Jana frowned curiously. Possibly there had been children of the liaison between that long ago Vincella and his charming little mistress, but if there had it would hardly be likely to concern the present generation, so she was quite frank with her question.

'A likeness to you?' she asked, but Francesca was laughing and shaking her head. 'I thought perhaps there were children and that you——'

'*No, no, no, cara,* I was not thinking of us at all.' She wiped the corner of her mouth lightly with her napkin and looked at her for a moment with a bright mischievous gleam in her eyes. 'I referred to her likeness to you, *bimba mia*; did you not notice it? Marco did!'

Jana swallowed the piece of roll she had just bitten off so hastily that it almost choked her, and she hastily picked up her knife to spread more honey on the rest of it so that the sweep of her hair hid her face for a few seconds, long enough for the sudden flush that coloured her cheeks to subside a little. She remembered all too vividly that Marco had said that Madonna Margherita was the kind of woman he could marry, and if he considered her like the Madonna—— She shook her head and gave Francesca a small uncertain smile.

'I can't say I noticed it,' she told her. 'Although I suppose the colouring is similar.'

'It is many years since I saw the painting,' Francesca mused, 'but I believe there is a likeness when I remember her, *cara*. She was a very pretty girl, no? Very—*delicata*.'

'Well, I'm definitely not delicate,' Jana told her with a rather unsteady laugh, 'so there the likeness ends, Francesca!'

There was a bright speculative gleam in Francesca's eyes as she got on with her meal that Jana found vaguely discomfiting, and she talked quickly as if she was hurrying to say what she wanted to say before they were interrupted. 'In Italian the word also means—dainty, *cara*, and you are so.' Francesca went on with her meal for a moment or two, but it was obvious she was thinking deeply about something still, and after a while she looked across at her and nodded firmly. 'I am sure that I have the best idea,' she declared as she carefully laid down her knife. 'And I think you will agree with me, Jana, when you hear!'

Jana smiled encouragingly, even though she had a curiously disturbing flutter of anticipation in her stomach that she did not yet see reason for. 'Tell me, and we'll see,' she told her.

Leaning her elbows on the table, Francesca took up her coffee cup and held it between her two hands while she talked, her eyes glowing with enthusiasm for her idea, whatever it was. 'I think that you must wear the disguise of Margherita Favoratini when you attend the *ballo di costume, cara mia*! It would be as if she had returned to life!'

Dark eyes flicked swiftly and critically over her face and she smiled. 'And it would please Marco if you did so,' she added softly.

Jana did her best to ignore the latter part of the remark, although it was difficult when Francesca so obviously expected some kind of reaction from her. As it was she took a moment to restore order to her rather confused thoughts, trying to imagine what Marco's reaction was likely to be to her appearing as a living version of his favourite painting. She had teased him about his obvious infatuation with the lady, and she wondered what he would make of her choosing that particular character for her costume.

'To please me you will be Margherita Favoratini, eh, Jana?' Francesca urged, and Jana shrugged after a moment or two and laughed.

'To please you?' She took another moment, then shrugged once more. 'I suppose I could, if you say there's a likeness. I haven't decided on anything yet. But I'd rather you didn't tell Stefano if you don't mind, Francesca.' She hesitated about being too pointed, but she had Stefano's idea of matching their costumes in mind. 'It's just that I'd rather we didn't go as a pair, if you know what I mean. It might give the wrong impression if he turned up as Gaspare Fabriano, the fourth Count.'

Francesca smiled and shook her head. 'I shall not say a word to Stefano, *cara*, I promise you. He will not appear as the fourth Conte di Vincella, you may be sure of it!'

Feeling strangely as if she had decided something much more important than her costume for the ball, Jana laughed and shook her head. 'That's settled, then—I go as Madonna Margherita.'

'Sì, it is settled,' Francesca agreed, obviously well pleased with her achievement. 'I will arrange for your costume and we will say not a word to anyone!' Jana finished her breakfast while Francesca continued to look thoughtful, apparently caught up in plans for the ball, until she looked across and caught Jana's eye suddenly and arched her brows curiously. 'Have you seen the picture of Margherita Favoratini's lover?' she asked, and so reminded Jana of her own intentions in that direction.

'Marco told me there was a painting of him here somewhere,' she told her. 'I didn't like to ask him too much because he seemed—I don't quite know—a bit reluctant to tell me too much about him. He said that he was known as the Eagle of the Vincella because he was such a ruthless man; he said he was very wealthy and successful and that he was about fifteen years older than his lady love, and that was about all.'

'But you are curious, hah?'

'Naturally, I'm curious,' Jana admitted frankly. 'I was going to ask you if you'd show me his portrait, but with the excitement of the engagement last night, it slipped my mind.'

Francesca glanced over her shoulder at the half-open door, to see if anyone was about to join them, she supposed, and Jana could not restrain a smile at the suggestion of intrigue. No wonder, she thought, though entirely without malice, that the Venetians had once been regarded as born intriguers!

'If you have finished your breakfast, Jana,' Francesca decided, 'we will go and seek out this ruthless and fascinating character, and you may decide for yourself!'

She led the way, along a gallery that branched off from the main one, and which Jana only vaguely remembered having seen before. It was lined with paintings, mostly portraits, and reminded Jana of the much smaller one at the Palazzo Favoratini; they had walked about half its length when Francesca brought her to a halt with a hand on her arm, pointing with the other hand to a large gilt-framed picture of a man.

'Gaspare Valentino Fabriano, fourth Conte di Vincella,' she said, with the same sense of drama that Marco had introduced his mistress with; and added with unexpected flippancy. 'Dishy, no?'

The use of such an adjective by someone like Francesca had the effect of making Jana want to giggle suddenly, but she had to agree that it was justly applied in the case of Gaspare Fabriano. He had the same kind of classic good looks that Stefano had, but there was a more ruthless line to the well-shaped mouth that was perhaps more reminiscent of Marco, and a touch of sensuality in the lower lip that she had noticed on occasion in both the cousins.

His eyes were coal black and stared out at the viewer from beneath straight black brows that just hinted at a frown, and his black hair was drawn back from his face and fastened at the back of his head, but long enough at the sides to cover his ears and slightly, very slightly, curled.

The coat he wore was dark red, ornately embroidered with gold and opened to reveal a grey silk waistcoat and a white shirt with a plain stock. The dark red with that darkly good-looking face gave him a certain dangerously Mephistophelean fascination that Jana found irresistible, and she stood and gazed at him for several moments before she felt Francesca's light touch on her arm and turned to smile at her.

'Is this how Margherita saw him, do you suppose, Francesca?' she asked, and Francesca shrugged.

'*Naturalmente, cara*, he would be about thirty-five years when this was painted, and she would have known him for five years.' Dark eyes studied her from the concealment of thick lashes and a smile hovered about her mouth. 'She had been his mistress for three of those years, so she would have known him very well, hah?'

Jana tried to imagine that gentle child in the little *palazzo* as mistress to the man who now gazed down at her with such arrogant confidence, and she could see the picture more clearly suddenly. She hadn't recognised the compassion in Marco's make-up until force of circumstances had brought it home to her, and perhaps a similar gentle streak had drawn Gaspare Fabriano to the dainty childishness of Margherita Favoratini; it was possible—it was probable, she decided.

'He's fascinating,' she said, reluctant to turn away. 'I think *I* could fall in love with a man like him too.'

Francesca smiled, as if she understood exactly what she meant. 'That is good,' she said softly, and Jana was too preoccupied for the moment to question her meaning.

CHAPTER NINE

IT was unbelievably quiet out there on the terrace, even allowing for the sound of the traffic of nearby canals, and the constant sound of bells in hundreds of campaniles all over Venice. The sun was warm, but Jana had found herself some shade and she was stretched out in a chair, with Stefano nearby apparently relaxed, but much less content with their present inactivity than she was herself.

She could see him if she just lifted her eyelids a fraction, and she noted that slightly sulky droop of his mouth with resignation. After walking around all week with Marco she found it refreshingly relaxing to sit out here on the terrace for an hour or so and just do nothing, but Stefano had wanted them to go off somewhere, as he usually did.

'Where have Giles and Francesca gone, do you know?' she asked him, mostly in an attempt to take his mind off feeling sorry for himself, and he shrugged carelessly.

'To Marghera, I think.'

Jana frowned curiously without opening her eyes. 'What would they go there for?' she asked. 'It's mainly industrial, isn't it? Francesca wouldn't be very interested in that, surely.'

Stefano saw it as an opportunity to bring his own situation to her notice once more, and he glanced across at her meaningly. 'Mamma goes wherever Giles wishes to go and does whatever he wishes to do because she likes to please him.'

'Unlike me, eh, Stefano?'

She smiled and sat up in her chair, looking at him with bright, teasing eyes so that he immediately left his chair and came to stand over her, taking her hands and holding them against his chest for a moment so that she could feel the vigour of his heartbeat and the warmth of his flesh beneath a silk shirt. There was a look in his eyes that sought to understand her attitude towards him, for he did not like it at all. He was unaccustomed to being at a loss where women were concerned, and he had never been sure of Jana.

Pressing her fingers close over his heart, he held them there determinedly. 'Do you not feel the way my heart beats for you?' he asked. 'Why do you not please me as Mamma does Giles?'

Feeling her senses in too much danger of responding to his nearness, she pulled her hands free and leaned back once more in her chair, eyes half-closed as she did so. 'Our situation is quite different, Stefano; I've no reason to follow you blindly wherever you choose to go.'

'As you do Marco!'

Only her heart beat betrayed anything at the mention of Marco, and outwardly she remained cool and unaffected. 'I work with Marco,' she reminded him. 'And he keeps me very busy, that's why I'm being lazy today; I'm quite happy sitting out here and doing nothing, Stefano, I really am.'

Disgruntled, he flopped back into his chair and sat with one hand supporting his chin, casting her long reproachful looks whenever she glanced in his direction. 'We are soon to be cousins,' he reminded her, and Jana opened her eyes a little wider, puzzled to know what track he was following now. 'I would think it would make you wish to be—nice to me.'

Under no delusion about just how nice he wanted her to be, Jana still tried to make her answer as gentle as possible, for she had no wish to hurt him no matter what he said or did. As a cousin she would like him very much, but she had no inclination for any closer relationship with him. 'I think

I *am* nice to you, in a cousinly kind of way, Stefano,' she told him. 'But I can't make myself feel something that just isn't there; I'm sorry, but it doesn't work like that.'

'Have you tried very hard, *carissima*?' The now familiar edge of harshness betrayed the first signs of anger, but she shook her head firmly.

'Please don't make a major issue of my wanting to sit out here and be lazy, Stefano,' she said, and closed her eyes once more. 'I simply don't want to go *anywhere*.'

'Unless it is with Marco, eh?'

She recognised the old cry yet again, one she had heard so often from him, and one she was beginning to believe was more true than he realised. It was four weeks since Giles and Francesca became engaged, and she could still recall that startling crack of breaking glass and the blood-red wine spilled over the white cloth by Marco's violent anger.

An anger that had without doubt been aroused in part by Stefano's attempt to make a mockery of Giles' announcement, but also, Jana was forced to recognise, by those unmistakable suggestions concerning her. Stefano's jibe about his being jealous had given her food for a great deal of thought during the past four weeks, although she still could not believe it was true. They worked together still, although the project was almost completed, and they had lunched together once or twice but she dared not look for anything other than his normally cool and mockingly gentle attitude in the way he treated her.

Rather than answer Stefano's question she pulled herself out of her chair and sat on the edge of it while she looked at him resignedly. 'All right,' she said with a rueful smile, 'if you want to go out, I'll go, but I shan't walk very far, I warn you, Stefano!'

He was on his feet in a minute and taking her hands he pulled her to him, bending his head to kiss her hard on her

mouth, almost as if he reprimanded her for being so reluctant to go with him. He seemed to have been more restless
than ever since his mother's engagement to Giles, and she
wondered if he was perhaps a little jealous of the attention
her uncle was getting, for Francesca had been a doting
mother, and particularly so since his father's death.

'Stefano——' Not quite sure of what she wanted to say,
she was nevertheless driven on by something she did not
quite understand as he stood holding her hands. 'You
don't—you don't *mind* Francesca marrying again, do you?
I mean, you don't dislike Giles, or the idea of him becoming
your stepfather?'

He looked at her for a moment, then shrugged. 'I do not
dislike Giles,' he decided after a moment or two. 'In fact I
quite like him, but I do not see why Mamma has to marry
him.'

Reminded of his suggestions regarding herself, Jana
frowned and there was a touch of asperity in her voice when
she questioned him; a gleam in her eyes that he viewed
warily. 'Are you suggesting the same kind of—arrangement
that you had in mind for you and me?' she asked. 'What is
it, Stefano? Don't you consider Giles and me good enough
for the Abrizzi?'

'Oh, Jana!' Clearly he had not expected such a response
and it was clear that he felt at least a little ashamed of the
impression he had given. Holding her hands tightly, he
looked down into her face. 'I do not pretend, Jana—with
you and me——' He shrugged and put it all in a nutshell,
very neatly. 'You are a beautiful girl, *carissima*, but I do
not feel for you in the way of a husband—I have the
passion for you, you understand?'

'Oh yes, I understand very well!' It was impossible not
to smile, however wryly. 'But I can't see why you should
think that Giles and Francesca come into the same cate-
gory. They truly love one another.'

Raising her fingers to his lips, he kissed their tips lightly, and there was a glimpse of that irrepressible mischief in his dark eyes when he looked down at her. 'It must be very true, *carissima*, for Mamma to give up so much!'

Now he had left her completely in the dark, and she could not even pretend to understand what he meant. Shaking her head slowly, she looked up at him and frowned. 'You mean her social life?' she asked. 'I admit Giles isn't a very social person, but perhaps Francesca is prepared to settle down a bit now——'

'And lose more than two-thirds of her income, *cara*?' He shook his head and drew a breath in between pursed lips. 'I would not do so much for any woman, *cara mia*!'

His dark eyes were watching her closely and she realised how much her expression told him. She had no idea, even now, exactly what it was he was telling her, but it was beginning to dawn on her, and she felt a sudden glow of affection for the woman her uncle was to marry. Drawing her hands from Stefano's, she walked off to stand looking down over the balustrade at the courtyard below, and the worn stone head of the Vincella eagle, her heart beating extra fast as she considered what he had said.

'Are you telling me,' she said, when she had sufficient control over her voice to sound cool and collected, 'that Francesca is giving up part of her income to marry Giles?'

'That is it precisely, *cara*.' He came and stood beside her, looking down into the shadowed courtyard and the quiet backwater beyond the arched gateway. 'In Papa's will he left everything equally between Mamma and me, including the shares in Abrizzi International, but the situation changes as soon as she remarries. Then she has only a modest income for the rest of her life. Papa did not wish anyone but an Abrizzi to be in control of Abrizzi International, you see—Mamma's shares come to me when she marries Giles.'

There was, Jana supposed a little dazedly, some kind of

practical sense in ensuring that family pride always remained uppermost, but it seemed very hard on Francesca to
make her choose between permanent widowhood and comparative poverty. She must love Giles very much indeed to
give up so much, and she felt a very warm affection for her
new aunt-to-be.

'I wonder if Giles knows,' she said, knowing how touched
her uncle would be if he thought his bride was sacrificing so
much for him. He might even feel he should give her a
second chance to change her mind, although from what she
knew of Francesca, she was unlikely to.

'Would it make a difference if he did?' Stefano asked,
and she straightened up to look at him narrow-eyed and
indignant.

'You don't know Giles at all if you think it would even
enter his head to marry Francesca simply because she was
wealthy,' she told him in a not quite steady voice, and
Stefano shrugged, deliberately careless, she suspected.

Straightening up himself, he stood beside her for a moment, darkly autocratic and uneasily reminiscent of Marco,
although Jana tried not to recognise it. 'Why would he
not?' he asked, and she looked at him for a moment trying
to fathom what was going on behind that smoothly good-
looking façade.

'Would *you*?' she challenged, and Stefano thought for a
moment, then shrugged once more with the same careless
ease.

'Quite probably,' he admitted, then hurried on almost as
if he had read something into her expression before she
realised it herself. 'And do not delude yourself, *carissima*,
that my cousin would be any less practical. Marco too
would choose to have a wealthy wife and a beautiful
mistress, and so have the best of two worlds. The Vincellas
have always been practical, Jana, and the present generation are no different!'

Jana looked down steadily at the smooth pate of the stone eagle and clenched her hands tightly on the balustrade. Maybe Marco was as mercenary as Stefano suggested, but she closed her eyes for a moment and determinedly conjured up the memory of his face and the softness of his voice when he had vowed that Margherita Favoratini was the kind of woman he could marry—or maybe he wasn't.

It was scarcely credible that the weeks had gone by so quickly, and Jana sat in front of her dressing-table mirror looking at her reflection with unseeing eyes; looking inward rather, at the events of the past weeks. She had come to Venice with the expectation of staying perhaps three or four weeks, perhaps even less, and their stay now had run into a full three months.

Her future, when she returned to England, was still a little uncertain, for she had not planned anything yet. Giles and Francesca were to be married in two days' time, with Marco as best man and Stefano giving away the bride; but Jana had not thought beyond that except at odd moments, and then, when she raised the subject with Giles he referred her to Francesca, who merely murmured softly in Italian and advised her not to worry about anything.

In the circumstances it was not too surprising to realise that she had acquired some of her new aunt's Latin fatalism and learned to shrug off the question whenever it came to mind. It was, however, becoming increasingly difficult to pretend she did not think about leaving the Palazzo Vincella with incredible reluctance; and the Conte di Vincella in particular.

She focused her attention on her own reflection once more and could not help but admire Francesca's skill in recreating the picture in the Palazzo Favoratini. Even the olive green brocade of the dress was an exact replica, as near as Jana could remember, and the open robe swept back to show a petticoat of gold damask supported by small side hoops.

The neck was low, much lower than she had realised, and it showed off the soft swell of her breasts so that she occasionally put a hand to her throat to cover for a moment the unaccustomed cleavage. The sleeves came to just below her elbows and were trimmed with braid, like the neckline; and the small lace cap that covered her high-piled hair might have been the very same one that Madonna Margherita wore.

Francesca's hairdresser had styled her hair to her client's instructions, and Francesca had been in to check on the finished product, then left her with instructions not to be too long in coming down, and not to forget to wear her *maschera*, the small black silk mask that covered her face from brow to nose and gave her, she decided as she studied her reflection once again, a very different view of herself.

She got up from the stool in front of the mirror and took a last look at herself, then turned with a trace of a sigh to move across the room in a rustle of silk petticoats, feeling almost sick with excitement and nerves. The very size of the gathering made her apprehensive, for she could not see herself at ease among such a motley throng of international celebrities as Francesca and Stefano had gathered together.

Her legs felt weak and they trembled alarmingly as she went along the gallery. She was quite late in the circumstances because she had delayed her appearance as long as possible, and she could hear the first revellers already enjoying themselves in the *sala grande* downstairs, a room she had not been into since that first evening when Francesca and Stefano arrived and they had dined in baroque splendour because Marco had been in a mood to amuse his old friend. The nervousness she had felt that night, when she broke a glass and cut her hand, was nothing to the way she felt now as she made her way downstairs, and she made the journey down the wide marble staircase last as long as possible.

Giles had been persuaded, heaven knew how, to don the guise of Julius Caesar, while Francesca complemented him as an extremely glamorous Cleopatra. She had no idea what disguises Marco or Stefano had chosen, for she had continued to keep the secret of her own costume from Stefano and she hoped Francesca had too. Even the vast tiled hall that she had crossed so many times in the past three months or so seemed to have taken on a new face, for it had a new warmth and animation as it echoed to the music and voices from the *sala grande*, every brilliant chandelier alight and glittering in its own light. It had come to life again, to its old splendour.

Nervously Jana smoothed down the green brocade and made sure her mask was in place, thanking heaven for the anonymity of it; until she was more sure of herself it would serve as something to hide behind. The room being fairly crowded already made it easier for her to slip in virtually unseen, for Francesca was busy greeting newcomers, and Giles she could see talking animatedly to a tall figure in a costume that struck Jana at once as familiar, although she did not immediately identify it.

Recognition came in the same instant that Francesca spotted her and glanced quickly behind her, saying something to the man with her uncle. In a moment the unmistakable figure of Gaspare Fabriano, the fourth Conte di Vincella, detached himself from her uncle's company and came towards her, and Jana's heart gave a wild, sickening lurch at the prospect of seeing that ruthlessly fascinating ancestor of Marco's brought to life.

Her next reaction, following closely on the first, was one of disappointment because obviously Francesca had told Stefano after all what her costume was to be, and he had devised his own to complement it. She could not altogether blame him, she thought as he made his way towards her, for the fourth Count had the same kind of classic good looks he had himself, and he was as much Stefano's ancestor as he was Marco's.

While he made his way through the people towards her Jana took note of the costume itself and could not help but admire the suitability of it and the attention to detail. A black silk mask hid the top half of his face, but she noted the deep red coat faced with gold embroidery and worn over a waistcoat of grey silk, just as in the portrait, with a white shirt and the plain stock at the neck. Red satin breeches and white stockings with black, buckled shoes were new to her because she had seen Gaspare Fabriano only as far as his waist, but the effect was like seeing that fascinating portrait come to life, and she did not for a moment realise that she had the same effect herself on the man who, when he reached her side at last, stood for a moment before he reached for her hand and raised it to his lips.

It took only a second, once he was close enough for her to be more aware of the man inside the clothes than the clothes themselves, to recognise that it was not Stefano who stood regarding her with that faintly quizzical look, but Marco, and when she realised it, she tipped back her head and laughed—in relief, she realised dazedly. He still held her hand, his long brown fingers curved tightly around hers, and the eyes behind the half-mask gleamed like jet, as if he too appreciated a situation that could surely not be a coincidence.

'Jana!'

He said it so softly that it was little more than a whisper, and it had a different sound from anything she had heard before, so that she felt a curious little tremor of sensation ripple along her spine as she looked up at him. Wearing the mask it was surprisingly easy to look directly at him, almost as if she was hidden, and he could only guess she was there behind it.

'How do you know?' she asked, then glanced briefly across at Francesca who, she thought, looked much too pleased with herself. 'Francesca told you,' she guessed, and could not pretend she minded that it was Marco she had told and not Stefano. 'She——'

'No one told me, *carissima*,' he interrupted swiftly, and using the endearment with such easy familiarity that she heard her own breath catch in her throat. 'No one had to tell me, Jana, I observed the likeness to Madonna Margherita when we visited the *palazzo*. The colouring is the same, and the eyes.'

'Oh, not the eyes, surely,' Jana teased breathlessly. 'I don't look as shy and sweet as Margherita, Marco, but the colouring is the same; I realised it when Francesca pointed it out to me.'

A faintly sardonic smile showed on his mouth and gleamed at her from the slits in the mask. 'Just as she so casually suggested that I should take on the disguise of the fourth Conte di Vincella,' Marco told her, and laughed softly while his long fingers squeezed her hand. 'I could not imagine why it was she saw *me* as the Count instead of Stefano; he is far more like him than I am, do you not agree?'

Jana was about to answer him when she noticed a courtly Spanish Don advancing upon them with unmistakable intent, and shook her head. 'Not in his present disguise,' she told Marco, and he turned and frowned.

'Jana, *cara mia*!' The manner was Stefano's even though the tall, bearded Spanish Don looked older than his twenty-two years, and the way he took her hand defied her companion to object. 'You have promised me this dance, *sì*?'

Jana had, she remembered vaguely, promised to have the first dance with him, and she looked up at Marco with the regret she felt showing quite unmistakably in her eyes. He let go her hand, his fingers sliding along her inner arm and leaving a shivering flutter on her skin, as Stefano turned her about, towards the dance floor.

'I won't be long, Marco.'

She realised as she was swept against the velvet firmness of a black doublet that she had taken it for granted Marco would be awaiting her return, when in fact he was probably not concerned at all. Stefano held her tightly, and from the eye-slits in his mask his dark eyes gleamed down at her. 'So,' he said, almost before they began dancing, 'You were not so secretive with Marco, eh, *carissima*?'

'I didn't tell Marco anything,' Jana denied firmly. 'And it wouldn't really concern you if I had, Stefano. I hope you're not going to be quarrelsome, I wanted to enjoy myself.'

'With Marco, I presume, hah?'

'Oh, I don't know!' She held herself stiff in his arms as they danced and wished she had refused to dance with him, no matter if she had promised or not. 'Stefano, please don't try and make me argue with you—I don't want to, but I can't keep—keep putting you off all the time. Please just dance with me and then let me go!'

'If that is what you wish, *ragazza*, then I *will* let you go! I am not prepared to regard myself as second best to my cousin—ever!'

Jana was left, stunned and not quite believing it had happened, in the middle of the crowd of dancers, while Stefano strode off in long angry strides and disappeared from her view before she recovered her breath. People around smiled, and it was so difficult to know whether or not they were smiles of encouragement or derision; below those uniform black masks it was so difficult to tell. But she felt very small and very angry as she pushed her way through to the edge of the floor on legs that felt barely capable of sustaining her weight.

Near the edge of the whirling crowd of dancers she caught a brief glimpse of a red and gold coat and grey silk waistcoat; caught the swift upward turn of a masked face and hurried on when she recognised Marco dancing with a boldly costumed harem beauty. There was no one near the door, but just before she reached it someone came up beside her and took her arm.

'*Signorina? Vuole ballare?*'

It was automatic to shake her head rather dazedly when she was asked to dance, but then, seeing his obvious disappointment, she nodded instead. Just because Stefano had behaved badly there was no reason why she should let him spoil the rest of the evening for her. He was a good dancer, whoever he was, and she thought he would have asked her to dance with him again, but someone else laid claim to her almost as soon as the music started and she was whirled off once more into the gaudy mêlée of costumed dancers.

Her costume was hot, hotter than she had anticipated, and she was in the act of shaking her head at another would-be partner when she was seized by her right wrist in long hard fingers that gripped her inescapably. 'Must I wait the whole evening to dance with you?' Marco asked, and she laughed breathlessly as she looked up at him.

Behind his mask she detected a glimpse of the familiar arrogance, as if he had every right to take her away from the man who now shrugged resignedly before going off to find another partner. Watching him go, she wondered what impression he had of Marco's possessive claim.

'You could have had the first dance,' she told him in a small and slightly unsteady voice. 'I was discarded like the proverbial old glove!'

The dark eyes watched her through elongated slits in the mask and they were steady and curious. 'Did Stefano truly walk away from you, as Francesca says?' he asked, and Jana nodded. 'Why, Jana? Why did he behave like that— what reason had he?'

Glancing up swiftly at his face, she unconsciously angled her chin. 'You think I gave him a reason, is that it?' she asked, and he smiled, one black brow arched upward above the rim of his mask.

'Who else, *piccina*?' His fingers had eased their hold on her wrist and now smoothed gently over her soft skin in a caress she found increasingly affecting. 'What did you quarrel about, *cara mia*?'

She did not want to tell him that they had not actually, that Stefano had purely and simply been jealous of him, Marco, and had been so angry that he stalked off and left her there on the dance floor alone. 'I don't think I want to tell you,' she decided at last, and his fingers once more tightened their grip. 'I thought you wanted to dance!'

He stood for a moment looking down at her and Jana could feel the incredible urgency of her heartbeat as she bore his scrutiny, then he started towards the door into the hall, taking her along with him, the strong fingers on her wrist irresistible even had she wanted to resist. '*Vieni!*' he commanded, but made no explanation, offered no reason why she should go with him.

'Marco——'

She glanced back over her shoulder as they crossed the hall, at the crowded *sala* and the whirling kaleidoscope of colourful costumes, but she offered no resistance, only did her best to keep pace with him as he took her towards the wide marble staircase. It crossed her mind briefly to wonder if the fourth Count Vincella could possibly have been any more single-minded in the pursuit of his own ends than the present holder of the title was.

'Marco, please, I can't keep pace with you!'

He turned, his eyes gleaming and his mouth showing a

hint of the mockery that always made her reproach him. 'You are once again accusing me of making you go too fast, *diletta*?'

The endearment was much more intimate than anything he had used before and Jana caught her breath, her lips slightly parted as she coped with her breathlessness. 'You're always in such a hurry,' she reproached him, and he laughed.

Coming to a halt part way along the gallery, he turned her to face him, then bent to kiss her mouth with a force that made her head spin. '*Sì, carissima mia*, I am in a hurry,' he told her, and kissed her again, lightly and gently so that she shivered. 'Come, let us go and look at the moon, eh?' Dark brown eyes coaxed irresistibly. 'Jana?'

He tucked her into the curve of his arm as he started once more along the gallery, and she was aware of the vigour of his body in such close proximity, conscious of a thousand and one sensations whirling through her senses until she was hardly aware of where she was. But it was to the main *sala* on the first floor, she could almost have guessed it, she thought, slightly light-headed as she crossed the big room still held close to him.

Many times she had imagined the scene; the *palazzo* bright and noisy with people and music, lights blazing, and these tall elegant windows set wide to the panorama of moonlit rooftops and distant spires. To the softness of summer nights, and the past generations of the Vincella bringing their lovers out on to this very same balcony to look at the city by moonlight; just as Marco was bringing her.

The air was warm and silky on her bare flesh, and she tried to bring some glimmer of practicality to a situation that rapidly was becoming more dreamlike than real. They walked to the very edge of the balcony, just above the looming menace of the Vincella eagle, and after looking out over the moonlit roof-tops for a second or two, Marco turned and looked into her face.

'You quarrelled with Stefano?' he said, not really asking her, although she nodded silently. 'About what, *carissima mia*?' Dark eyes gleamed at her from the slits in the black mask and she saw the promise there of the same passion that had thrilled her once before, though this was not aroused by anger. 'What did you say to him, *carina*, eh?'

'He thought I'd—arranged with you to wear these particular two costumes,' she said in a breathlessly unsteady voice. 'He wouldn't believe I hadn't, and he was angry. He also said he would never——' she hesitated, glancing upward at that masked face with its dark gleaming eyes, then the words came, too quickly and breathlessly soft. 'He said he would never regard himself as second best to his cousin.'

'Had it been suggested that he was—second best to his cousin?' Marco asked with remarkable quietness, and Jana once more glanced up at him before she answered.

'Not in so many words,' she said, and caught her breath when a long hand slid beneath her chin and raised her face to the bright, revealing moonlight. 'I think he thought——'

Jana got no further than that, for she was turned into the circle of Marco's arms and held there so firmly she had little hope of moving away and the easiest thing was to lift her arms and put them around his neck. Her heart thudded urgently hard and her whole body responded to the irresistible nearness of him as he gathered her even closer in his arms and bent his head until his face filled her vision, the eyes dark and stunningly bright behind the unfamiliar mask.

An impatient hand whisked it away, leaving the black hair disturbed and untidy, falling over his brow until Jana reached with light fingers and brushed it back. Then her own mask was removed, more gently and slowly, leaving her feeling oddly vulnerable without it, and his mouth came down to claim hers, gentle at first, belying that gleaming passionate darkness in his eyes, then harder and more fiercely until she felt herself deprived of all sense of time and conscious action.

Every fibre of her body responded to him; to the demands he made on her body and on her senses, and she could almost believe she had been taken out of this world and transported to another. She had known she loved him; ever since he had watched her go with Stefano for that first dance, she had known that, perhaps even longer, but what she felt now was something much more heady and exciting.

'Marco; oh, my love!' Her eyes closed she pressed her cheek to his, while his lips brushed lightly on her neck, his breath stirring her bright hair.

'I love you, *carissima mia*; I love you so very much, and I was too fearful of saying it too soon for fear I——' He laughed, that soft deep sound she found so affecting, and hugged her close while he kissed her mouth once more, almost taking the breath from her body. 'I wish to marry you, *piccina*; will you be my wife?'

Looking up at him, Jana's eyes had the deep blueness of sapphires, but the moonlight gave them a dark shadowy softness that made them as huge as a child's. 'Stefano said you never would—marry me,' she hurried on when he frowned at her. 'He said you were practical like all the Vincellas, like they'd always been. You'd marry a wealthy wife and have a beautiful mistress, he told me.'

'*Dio mio!*' Marco swore. 'What does he know of my heart; of my plans? Did I not tell you, *diletta mia*, that I could marry a woman like Madonna Margherita? And have I not said that you are like her?' He drew her close once more and kissed her mouth, long and hard until Jana felt she would never breathe again. 'What does Stefano know?' he asked softly. 'I will marry you, *carissima mia*, because I love you, and I marry whom I please!'

Jana smoothed her hands over the dark red coat of his costume and smiled, remembering the man in the portrait. 'And because you're the Eagle of the Vincella, as he was?' she asked.

'Sì, piccina! For tonight I am the fourth Conte di Vincella and you are his lovely little mistress, eh, diletta mia? For tonight we will give their love story a very different ending.' His arms held her more tightly and she lifted her face to him once more. 'Will you marry me, Jana carissima mia?'

'I love you, how can I say anything but yes?' Jana asked softly, and lifted her mouth to him once more.

It was minutes later, when she looked down over the balustrade and on to the head of the stone eagle hovering there in the moonlight, that she remembered that other, more opulent figure locked away in the strongroom downstairs; the guardian of the Vincella fortunes, according to Francesca. Lifting her head from Marco's broad chest, she looked up into his face, her eyes shadowed.

'Marco—what will you do about the Eagle——' She glanced briefly at the one above the portico. 'I mean the golden one. You won't——'

'No, diletta mia, I will not part with it—it is for my sons; I cannot part with their inheritance!' He raised her face to him and kissed her flushed cheeks, then her mouth, long and lingeringly, looking down into her face for a moment before he shook his head. 'Now let us go back to the party, eh, carissima?'

Jana sighed regretfully, looking out at the moonlit setting of Venice and the dreamy confusion of spires and cupolas and winding serpents of dark water. 'I suppose we must,' she agreed, and Marco bent and kissed her mouth, laughing softly as he turned her into the big sala once more.

'We must,' he agreed, his arm tightly around her. 'I have an announcement to make!'

The Warrender Saga

The most frequently requested series of Harlequin Romances . . . Mary Burchell's Warrender Saga

<table>
<tr><td>A Song Begins</td><td>The Curtain Rises</td></tr>
<tr><td>The Broken Wing</td><td>Song Cycle</td></tr>
<tr><td>Child of Music</td><td>Music of the Heart</td></tr>
<tr><td colspan="2" align="center">Unbidden Melody</td></tr>
<tr><td colspan="2" align="center">Remembered Serenade</td></tr>
<tr><td colspan="2" align="center">When Love Is Blind</td></tr>
</table>

Each complete novel is set in the exciting world of music and opera, spanning the years from the meeting of Oscar and Anthea in *A Song Begins* to his knighthood in *Remembered Serenade*. These nine captivating love stories introduce you to a cast of characters as vivid, interesting and delightful as the glittering, exotic locations. From the tranquil English countryside to the capitals of Europe— London, Paris, Amsterdam—the Warrender Saga will sweep you along in an unforgettable journey of drama, excitement and romance.